M000297784

A Mother's Day Murder

A Mt. Abrams Mystery

by
Dee Ernst

All the characters in this book are the product of an overactive imagination. Any resemblance to a real person, living or dead, is a tremendous coincidence.

Copyright 2015
235 Alexander St.

235
ALEXANDER
STREET

ISBN 13: 978-0-9970514-0-7

If you'd like to learn more about Mt. Abrams, including other books in the series, please visit
https://mtabrams.com

To find more of other Dee's books, go to
www.deeernst.com

Comments? Questions? An uncontrollable desire to just chat? You can reach me at
Dee@deeernst.com

CHAPTER ONE

MT. ABRAMS WAS exactly the kind of quaint, close-knit community that people dreamt about. Everyone knew everyone else, people smiled and rescued kittens, childhood sweethearts lived happily ever after, and everyone who lived there, when asked, would all say the same thing—"Yes, it's a lovely place to live. Nothing ever happens here."

Everyone who lived there was, of course, lying. Mt. Abrams was exactly the kind of quaint, close-knit community where everything and anything happened, quite often, and to lots of people. There were moms who drank too much wine, kids who did drugs and shoplifted makeup from Lord & Taylor, adultery, vicious gossip (much of it true) and worse.

We all thought that a certain wife kept falling down the stairs way too often. And the single mom with the drug problem kept sending her kids away to her "grandparents," and we all smiled and nodded and ignored the child services worker who came every week. And, of course, there were "characters." As my very good friend Shelly Goodwin often said, Mt. Abrams seemed to have a disproportionately high percentage of drunks, assholes, and whack jobs.

But the myth persisted. Nothing ever happened there.

Until Lacey Mitchell dropped off the face of the earth.

For me, Ellie Rocca—divorced, working from home, and in a little bit of a rut—it became almost a challenge to figure out where she'd gone, and more importantly, why.

Routine meant a lot to the people around here. Just like any small town, people liked things to stay pretty much the same from day to day, especially when kids were involved. The morning bus stop ritual, for example, was sacred. So when Lacey Mitchell did not walk with her boys to the bus stop one Monday morning, we all noticed. Lacey usually stood with her two sons, David and Jordan, smiling faintly from a short but significant distance from the main group. That morning, her husband Doug did the honors. I smiled and waved, and immediately started to wonder—laziness? Doing her roots?

"Hi, Doug, is Lacey all right?" I called over. He was standing as far away from the bus stop as was humanly possible without actually being on another block.

The two boys both turned and looked up at their father.

"She's fine," Doug said. He smiled briefly. "Her father is ill. In Buffalo. I drove her to the train station Saturday."

Jordan, the older of the boys, tugged on Doug's sleeve and muttered something, but Doug shook him off without even glancing down at his son. "Don't know how long she'll be away."

I nodded. "Oh. Well, give her my best when you talk to her. Do you need any help with the boys?"

Doug flashed another smile. "No, thanks, ah, um…"

"Ellie," I reminded him.

Another tight smile. "Right. Ellie. We're good."

I turned back to the circle of moms, eyebrows raised. "Buffalo?" I whispered.

"I never realized she had a father in Buffalo," Sharon Butler said.

"I never realized she had parents, period," Shelly Goodwin muttered, and the group burst into smothered laughter.

"Come on," I said. "Lacey isn't that bad."

Maggie Turner made a noise. "Yes, she is. She's like a mom-bot, all perfect and polite. Him too. They're like Stepford people."

She did have a point. They were a beautiful couple—tall, lean and vaguely Nordic, with fair hair and pale blue eyes. They both had a certain look, as though they'd met while modeling for Abercrombie & Fitch. They looked like the type of people you couldn't imagine doing anything even vaguely distasteful, like throwing up in the back seat of a car. Their sons were equally good looking and polite, and managed to never get their clothes dirty.

The bus pulled up, and the sounds of the engine and cries of good-bye drowned out all conversation. I gave ten-year-old Tessa a kiss and waved as my beautiful, fearless, and way-too-stubborn little girl climbed on the bus.

The bus chugged up the hill, and I turned to Shelly. "Ready?"

Shelly nodded. "In fifteen?"

I nodded and watched as Doug got into his Camry to drive away, and then trudged up the hill to home. In fifteen minutes I'd be back down with Boot, the most spoiled cocker spaniel in the world, and a Thermos mug of coffee for a morning walk around Mt. Abrams. It was all the exercise I got these days, and since I was on the slow rise after fifty, I made the effort, even on days not as perfect as this beautiful May morning.

When I came through the door into my kitchen, there was no blare of hip-hop or garbled television noise from upstairs. Cait was still asleep. Caitlyn was my other beautiful, fearless, way-too-stubborn daughter. She was twenty-four. She was born in the first years of my marriage, when things between Marc and I had been great. Tessa was born in the last few years of the same marriage, when sex was the only thing Marc and I had left in common. Now Marc lived in a sleek two-bedroom condo in Hoboken with a view of the New York skyline. I was still in a slightly shabby, decidedly quaint Victorian on Abrams Lane, around the corner from the post office and town library, with a view of the lake.

Cait had just finished a very expensive graduate program with a master's degree in French poetry, with a specialization in early nineteenth century romantics. I figured she'd be switching from her part-time job waiting tables at a chichi French restaurant to a full-time job waiting tables at a chichi French restaurant any day now.

I filled my Thermos with hot coffee, then added way too much sugar and flavored creamer, and called for Boot. She skittered around the corner into the kitchen, ears perked, stump tail wagging. Boot is milk white with black spots and a single black paw. She sat patiently while I attached her leash. My phone made its *You've Got Mail* noise. A text from Carol Anderson. She'd meet me at the corner.

Carol was ten years older than I, with all her kids grown and mercifully out of the house. She'd lived in Mt. Abrams all of her life, having been born in one of the Victorian houses on the top of the hill, and then having moved into a more spacious Craftsman-style house after her marriage. She knew all the old guard, and as the librarian at our tiny local branch, she knew many of the newer residents as well.

I bet she'd know something about Lacey Mitchell.

"She rents lots of movies for the boys," Carol said. "Superhero stuff. She reads mostly nonfiction. I never see him at all." Carol treated her relationships with library patrons with the same confidentiality as a doctor or lawyer, often claiming you could tell more about a person from what they read than by any other means. She kept everyone's guilty secrets intact, for the most part, but was not above breaking her code of silence for a good cause. "Last week she came in on Thursday. That's the last time I saw her." She glanced down at me. "Father in Buffalo?"

I nodded. I never talked much when we walked. Carol was almost six feet tall and had legs up to her neck, and despite the few years she had on me, never seemed out of breath, even going uphill. Shelly was my height, almost five-six, but jogged everywhere and ran marathons in her spare time. I managed to keep up with them mostly because Boot pulled me up the hills, but trying to have a conversation anywhere but on a flat stretch of road was too much to ask, and both of them knew it.

We turned onto Morris, which was *almost* not a backbreaking incline. Shelly tugged on Buster's leash. Buster was a chocolate lab, and you'd think he'd love the great outdoors, but he hated the hills as much as I did.

"I bet there's something odd there," Shelly said. Shelly was five years younger than I, and my best friend in Mt. Abrams. Her youngest son was the same age as Tessa. I had met her during my first week in Mt. Abrams, when her previous chocolate lab, Bruno, wandered into my new house and refused to leave. Cait adopted him on the spot, and when Shelly arrived to claim her wayward pet, she had to resort to some quick thinking to get her back. Cait became her dog sitter.

I became her friend.

Shelly was average height with a flat body—no boobs, no butt, narrow hips. She was very healthy and fit and had a heart of pure gold.

Carol rolled her eyes. "There's always been something odd there. I mean, those kids come into the library and never speak unless spoken to. Not that I object. Those boys are model library citizens. But who has kids like that anymore?"

Maggie Turner came jogging out of her short driveway and ran around us, grinning. "Come on, Shel, let's take the next hill," she said.

Maggie was young, thirty-six, with way too much time on her hands when she was home. Her hair was bleached blonde, super short, and she had five visible tattoos. She was a professional musician, playing second violin in a fairly famous chamber group that gave concerts worldwide. When she was touring, during five or six months every winter, her husband Derek, an artist and cartoonist, cared for six-year-old Serif.

Who was a little girl, in case you were wondering. I know. Serif. That's a therapy session just waiting to happen.

Maggie was wearing high-cut gym shorts and a Guns N' Roses T-shirt. "Up the hill?"

Shelly tugged at Buster again. "Not today. What did you think of Doug?"

Maggie stopped bouncing and settled in beside Carol. "I think the two little boys were as surprised as we were about Lacey having a sick father."

I nodded. "Yeah, I noticed that too. And Doug looked awful, like he'd had no sleep."

Carol shrugged. "Maybe she left him. Maybe he threw her out. Maybe they were up all night having great monkey sex, and she couldn't walk this morning."

I was in the process of taking a gulp of coffee as she said that and spewed it all over the street. "Monkey sex?"

Carol nodded. "Yes. When you climb up the headboard, shrieking."

I licked coffee off my thumb. "Well, I wouldn't know about that. I've pretty much forgotten what sex is, even the non-monkey kind."

"Seriously, Ellie, I can introduce you to Martin," said Maggie. "He's first cello. Amazing guy."

I shook my head as we turned onto Davis Road. It was quiet and flat, lined with what looked to be Victorian dollhouses. Back in the late 1800s the lots had only been thirty feet wide at the street, so the homes were all narrow and deep, with tiny porches and lots of gingerbread trim. Kate Fisher was on her porch, as she was every morning. We waved and tried to hurry by, but we weren't quite fast enough. Kate was a talker.

"Ladies, good morning! Oh, I love spring, don't you? And this is the weekend I set out my impatiens. I hate to see the pansies go, but it's time…"

We walked on. Luckily, Kate never minded if no one answered her.

There were a few rental properties in Mt. Abrams. The general consensus was that renters did not make good neighbors because they didn't care how their properties looked. Even though she had only lived there a few weeks, Kate was quickly earning the respect of all of Davis Road. She'd painted all the trim of her tiny house herself, a bright white, and had filled all her window boxes with pansies. It was too bad she couldn't keep her mouth closed for more than seven seconds at a time.

We turned again, climbed another hill, and finally, spread out in front of us, was the lake. Beyond that rose the mountain that Josiah Abrams named after himself. My house was off to the left, across from the water. Josiah's original house had been expanded over the years to become the clubhouse, and come summer, the social center of Mt. Abrams. The Mitchell house stood on the opposite side of the lake, facing the clubhouse, looking pristine in the morning sun.

The whole vista was flushed with the first pale green of spring, and the reflection off the water was breathtaking.

I stopped to take it all in. I got to see this every single morning. What else could I want from life? Probably not a cello player. "No thanks, Maggie. I'm going to leave my love life to fate."

Shelly sighed. "Yeah. Good luck with that."

The community of Mt. Abrams was founded in 1871 by Josiah Milner Abrams, a Brooklyn-born merchant who made a fortune during the Civil War by supplying the Union army with saddles and bridles for its cavalry. He had grown tired of the city life, such as it was, so one day he got on the train in Hoboken and traveled due west into the untamed heart of New Jersey, looking for a little piece of paradise he could call his own.

Legend has it that when the train stopped at Lawrence Township, he stepped off to stretch his legs and started wandering up a nearby hill. He forgot all about getting back on the train, apparently overwhelmed by the natural beauty of the place. At the top of the hill was a crystal clear lake, and beyond that, a small mountain so green that Abrams fell in love and bought the whole shebang. Luckily for him, the small mountain was insignificant enough that it didn't have a name, so of course, he named it after himself. He started by building a grand summer retreat. He had dreamed of a quiet, private paradise for him and his family, but his heirs had other ideas, and most of them involved making more money by selling off everything Josiah had owned, including his land. By the time Marc and I looked at Mt. Abrams, it was your basic lakeside community. Quirky, yes, but hardly paradise.

When Marc and I moved there in the mid-nineties, he wanted a nice, modern bi-level, steps from the train station, so he could commute easily rather than try to drive every day into New York City. I fell in love with one of the original Victorians—not right on the lake, but close enough. Since living by the lake meant he had to walk ten minutes to the station instead of three minutes, he hesitated. Once he conceded that, from a resale perspective, lake view was a better location, we bought the house. Because it had been fairly neglected, we bought it for a song and spent five years in a state of continual rehabilitation. Not the best way to live, but Cait learned early on the joys of new sheetrock and that fresh paint smell.

I loved it. Marc did not. He tried, but he grew to hate the house—its quirky electrical system, uneven floors, and random fits of falling shingles. By the time Tessa was born he was done—with the house, the small-town living, and with me. He got a shorter commute. I got the house I'd always wanted, amazing friends I'd cultivated for years, and a king-size bed all to myself.

Small-town living isn't for everyone. I loved it. There was a real sense of community and safety that I felt comfortable with. I often left my door unlocked, and let Tessa walk to her friends' houses without any real worry. Caitlyn hated it. Everyone knew everything, she complained. People were always judging, she insisted.

And nothing ever happened.

CHAPTER TWO

WORKING FROM HOME had lots of advantages. I never had to worry about what to wear, for example, although some days I'd catch a glimpse of myself in the mirror and think that maybe, just maybe, I should rethink my usual uniform of yoga pants and T-shirts. But I needed to be comfortable. I was a freelance editor. I used to be a junior editor in a very well-known publishing house, right down the hallway from Marc's office. It was where we met, fell in love, and worked side by side for years. When Caitlyn was born, I took a few years off before returning a few days a week, then back to full time. Marc and I dropped Cait off at daycare and took the train to Penn Station together. I always took an earlier train home, got Cait, and began my second and third jobs as wife and mom. It worked out quite well for a long time, aside from the part where I was exhausted and grouchy and kept asking Marc when he was going to start to help around the house.

But after Tessa was born, several things happened at once. A larger conglomerate bought out my company, resulting in a huge promotion for Marc and a job elimination for me. Self-publishing started to pick up a little steam, and independent authors needed independent editors to work for them. And finally, Marc leaving forced me to rethink how I was going to support myself. Did I really want to find another NYC job?

So I went online and stalked writers boards and groups, and little by little, I started getting work. Self-pubbed authors had no real money, so I gave all my clients huge breaks on their first few manuscripts. Luckily, I managed to get quite a few good writers wanting my services, and soon they were making enough good money to start paying me good money. That, along with an excellent divorce lawyer, made me feel fairly secure moneywise. When my father died a few years ago, I got an insurance payment that allowed me to buy out Marc's share of the house and pay off most of the mortgage. I had no car payment anymore;

Cait's education had been paid for by grants and scholarships, and I even had a savings account in case the roof collapsed or the furnace blew up. Living in an old house made for a long list of possible emergency scenarios.

My life was good. I had few complaints. I was even getting a little restless and—dare I say it—bored. The problem was I specialized in mystery novels. Cozies, thrillers, classic whodunits—my mind was never more entertained than when the dead body showed up. And I was good at finding plot holes, making sure the red herrings weren't too obvious, and tying up all the ends nice and tight. I was an excellent editor, if I do say so myself, because my brain was very good at the little details that made for a first-class mystery. That made my real crime-free life a bit dull. That's probably why when I got home that morning I went straight to my computer to Google Lacey Mitchell.

Doug and Lacey Mitchell came to Mt. Abrams last year, moving into the old Dwight house after it sat empty for almost six years. There were a string of owners before them, each one doing less and less upkeep until it was a sad, shabby wreck of a place. When we saw the Mitchells putting all sorts of time and money into the house, we were all pretty excited. And when the last of the painters and landscapers drove away, and the Dwight house stood at last, gleaming white in the summer sun, we all waited breathlessly for the first of us to see what the interior looked like.

We were still waiting. We knew nothing more about the family than we did when they first moved in. Hopefully, that was about to change.

There were more Lacey Mitchells than I could have possibly imagined. I narrowed the search to Lacey Mitchells in New Jersey. Nothing. I tried to remember if anyone had found out where they had moved *from* when the family moved to town.

I texted Shelly. She managed a very busy allergist's office, but I knew she constantly checked her phone. Sure enough, after searching fruitlessly for fifteen more minutes, I got a text back.

I think VA

Good. Lacey Mitchell, Virginia, and bingo—there she was.

Lacey Scott Montgomery, of the Fairfax Montgomerys, married Douglas Wade Mitchell, on December 24, 2002.

Mr. Mitchell hailed from Austin, Texas, where he was employed as an engineer. Ms. Montgomery recently graduated from Sweet Briar with a degree in public relations.

Public relations? Lacey needed to go get her tuition money back. She'd obviously learned nothing about PR.

Then I Googled the Fairfax Montgomerys. Yes, Lacey did have a mother. Millicent Clair Montgomery, nee Wilcox. She also had a father but not anymore. I read the obituary very carefully. Gerald Montgomery had died the previous February. It happened suddenly. He was survived by his daughter Lacey and two grandsons.

Wait. Why wasn't the wife mentioned? Had they been divorced?

I looked around the Internet. I was on a mission. No mention of divorce or separation, but I wasn't sure something like that was open information. Last mention of Millicent was the wedding announcement, back in 2002. Nothing at all since, not even in a Lifestyle section where the comings and goings of the Fairfax elite were carefully documented. Millicent had simply vanished. Much like her daughter.

There was another little snippet about Gerald in what looked to be an even more local weekly paper. There, nestled among pie contest results and advertisements for John Deere tractors, was a little article about the generous Mr. Montgomery and how he had used his family money to better the community by donating to various charities, including the library and Habitat for Humanity.

Hmmm. Family money. According to the *Fairfax Bulletin* his family money was estimated to be in the neighborhood of five million dollars. And without the wife in the picture, could Lacey have inherited the whole bundle? I sat back and stared at the computer screen.

So much for sick in Buffalo.

"Mom. Are you working?"

"Of course," I lied. I'd been in the process of trying to see if ol' Gerald had probated his will, how much was involved, and most importantly, who got it all. I minimized the screen and stared intently at the incredibly tedious cozy mystery I was supposedly copyediting. "What's up?"

Caitlyn Elizabeth Symons looked exactly like I would have looked at twenty-four if I had been six inches taller with a discernible waist, shapelier butt, and boobs. And a better nose. And red hair. She had her father's eyes and my chin, which wasn't a bad thing. She was a very pretty girl with a smokin' hot body and a potty mouth that could put a longshoreman to shame. She was also very smart about all sorts of things, but not necessarily common sense things. She made, at one point in her high school career, a small solar rocket that placed third in a national science fair. But for God's sake, don't let her near an iron.

She walked into my office, which was a sunroom perched in a corner of the second floor directly over the porch, and sank into a battered but cozy armchair I'd stashed in the corner for when I needed to relax my brain. She was sipping coffee from a very large mug.

"Would you kill for five million dollars?" I asked her.

"Depends. Why, did Grandma strike it rich?"

"No." I swiveled in my office chair away from my computer to face her. "You'd kill Grandma?"

"Of course not. Who has five million dollars?"

"Lacey Mitchell. Her father died recently and may have left her a bundle."

"Is there anyone in our family to leave us a bundle?" she asked.

I shook my head. "Nope."

"Oh. So *we're* going to kill Lacey Mitchell?"

I shook my head again. "Nope."

She sighed. "Why do you start these conversations?"

"You came up here, remember? I repeat—what's up?"

"I applied for a fellowship in French comparative literature. They want me to go out for an interview."

I think my jaw dropped open. I never imagined she'd find anything that was even remotely related to her chosen field of study. But wait—would she get paid for something like that? "Cait, that's amazing! Oh, I'm so happy for you. When?"

"The first week in June."

"Where?"

"Catholic University."

I made a face. "Well you know how I feel about being Catholic, but if they're willing to take you anyway, that's just great. Where is that, D.C.?"

"Lyon."

I stopped being excited. "Lyon as in France?"

She nodded.

"Oh," I said.

My office has floor-to-ceiling windows on three sides, and long gauzy curtains diffuse most of the light, but I swear the world got a little bit darker there for a second. "You're going to France? They hate us in France. And it's very expensive there. Finding a place to live is going to be impossible. Don't you watch *House Hunters International*?"

"First of all, the French do not hate us. And I've been saving money like crazy. You know that. I haven't bought so much as a new pair of shoes in three years. I've got lots of money in the bank."

I took a deep breath. Oh, my dear, sweet little girl. She was a *waitress*. She only worked three nights a week. I mean, really, how much could she have saved? I stood up, stretched, and then gazed out the window. "Exactly how much have you got in that little nest egg of yours?"

"Eighteen thousand dollars."

I spun around to gape at her. "*What?*"

She looked at me patiently. "Mom, I've been working for seven years. Since high school."

"But part time."

"Still."

She waited. I knew what she was thinking.

During her junior year of high school when she should have been traveling around to all the out-of-state colleges she was determined to get into, Marc left. I was a mess. So was she, but for a different reason. She saw the writing on the wall just as clearly as I did. That was the summer she started working at Pierre's, and that was the summer she told me she could get just as good an education at Rutgers and live at home to save money, keep her part-time job, and help out with Tessa. So she'd commuted through a four-year BA, then a two-year masters program. She was done. I was no longer a quivering mass of depression and anger. Tessa was a serene and oddly mature child. Cait didn't need to be here anymore.

"Honey, they'll be lucky to have you. What an amazing opportunity. And you'll be able to live like a queen. Who knew?"

She flew out of the chair and into my arms, picking me up and hugging me tightly. "Oh, thank you, Mom. I was so afraid you'd freak out."

There were tears in my eyes. "I am freaking out. I will miss you terribly. But you deserve this."

She was crying too. "Yeah, I think so. So, which of us tells Tessa?"

Tessa only worshipped her older sister with a devotion formerly found in ancient apostles.

I shook my head. "Not me. This is your dance. You pay the piper."

She grinned. "Okay. I'll buy her pizza first."

I wiped the tears off my face. My little baby. All grown up at last and going off on her own. As much as she was often a huge pain in my butt, I knew I'd have a lot of emotional adjusting to do. "She'll want your room, you know."

Cait went back to sit back down, resuming her coffee sipping. "Well, she can't have it. Not yet. Now, who is this Lacey Mitchell person, and why do you think someone killed her for five million dollars?"

Cait's announcement distracted me from work—and Lacey Mitchell. We went out to lunch, stopped at the bank to take her passport out of the safety deposit box, and had our toes done. All that girlish bonding did little to make me feel any happier about the fact that my child, my firstborn baby, was going across the ocean to live in a strange country where even though she knew the language and loved the culture, she would be a complete outsider, alone, without her mother's advice and support.

"Mom, you know I rarely take your advice now," she reminded me, after I expressed my concern.

"I know. But I can give it to you. I can actually see you smile and nod. How can I do that when you're in France?"

"Skype."

Damn that kid. She had an answer for everything.

She dropped me off at the bus stop in Upper Main Park, then drove the car up the hill. It was about twenty minutes until Tessa came home from school, so I sat on a bench and quietly took in a truly beautiful spring day. The forsythia was in bloom, as were the daffodils. Birds were singing. A small bunny hopped across Marie Wu's front yard. I half expected a Disney princess to burst out from somewhere, singing at the top of her lungs and leading a conga line of dancing deer.

"So Ellie. What about Garden Club?"

Lynn Fahey probably worked for the CIA in a former life. She snuck up on me so suddenly I literally jumped.

"God, Lynn, wear a bell around your neck or something, please?"

She sat next to me, crossed her legs, and began bouncing her foot. She was always in motion. Barely over five feet tall, she was one of those aggressively busy women, running to meetings and organizing events. She was vice president of the Garden Club, a member of the Mt. Abrams Historical Society, was on the local PTA fundraising committee, and ran coffee hour at the Methodist Church. She also had two kids in middle school, and her husband always looked happy.

"I'm not joining the Garden Club, Lynn. For one thing, I don't have a garden." My house did have a yard, and there were things planted in that yard, but that had been Marc's doing. Cait weeded and watered things for me. I mowed the small patch of green that, I'm sure, contained a few blades of grass among the weeds. Tessa had a jade plant that I was trying desperately not to kill.

"You don't need a yard to be in the Garden Club, Ellie. You just need to love plants."

"I don't love plants, Lynn. I have a black thumb." I glanced at my watch. Eight more minutes until the bus.

Lynn tugged on the end of her braid. Her hair was long and light brown, barely streaked with gray. Her braid fell past her waist, adding to her hippie-chic fashion style. Today she was wearing faded jeans, a batik peasant-style blouse, six or seven long beaded necklaces, and Birkenstocks with argyle socks. "Ellie, please. Do you know what Mary Rose is planning? She wants to put pavers in the library park. Can you imagine?"

The library did not actually have a park. It did have a small grassy area by the entrance, where the Garden Club had planted a bank of hydrangeas a few years ago, and had recently installed a picnic table.

I could see Sharon Butler coming around the corner. Sharon was young, in her early thirties, with a six-year-old son. She was considerably overweight, probably close to two hundred and fifty pounds, but she trotted up the hill with a smile and no apparent shortness of breath.

"Honestly, Lynn, pavers aren't so terrible. It gets really messy around there in the winter."

That was obviously the wrong thing to say. Lynn and Mary Rose Reed were as close to archenemies as one got in Mt. Abrams. Their wildflower garden feud had been epic.

"Pavers would ice over, and that would mean salt being put down. Salt would get swept to the side, all over the hydrangeas, and would kill them off in just a few years. Do you really want to kill the hydrangeas?"

"Of course, not. So, you want me to join so I can become part of the anti-paver voting block?" Sharon, now within earshot, made a sympathetic face. Lynn's strong-arm tactics were the stuff of legend.

Lynn leaned over to give me a quick hug. "Exactly. Meeting is Thursday at seven-thirty. In the firehouse. See you there." She bounced up, waved at Sharon, and then disappeared as quickly as she had come.

Sharon laughed. "Did she recruit you? Pavers?" Sharon was very pretty, always perfectly made up, and her hair carefully colored and styled. She worked from home too, but managed to get herself dressed in coordinated outfits with matching accessories. Today her earrings and necklace complimented the blue in her cotton sweater. She also always wore perfume. I was a tad jealous.

I nodded. The rest of the moms materialized, and seconds later, the bus pulled to a stop. Tessa was first off the bus, of course. She liked being first. At anything and everything. I liked to think that having big sister fed into her competitive spirit.

David and Jordan Mitchell did not get off the bus. They were obviously hanging out at the Mt. Abrams Elementary School gym, along with all the other kids in the after-school program, including Shelly's boys. The program ran until six. I had often seen Doug pull in as late as eight in the evening. I wondered what other last-minute arrangements he'd had to make.

Tessa lifted her face for a kiss and handed me her backpack.

"Good day?" I asked.

She nodded, standing patiently and waiting until Jerome got off the bus. Jerome's mom, Jessica, dropped him off every morning, and Tessa and I walked him to Bev Sutter's house every afternoon, who watched him until Jessica picked him up after she got off work. There were a fair number of stay-at-home moms in Mt. Abrams, but living barely thirty miles west of New York City made for a fairly high cost of living, and most of the families had both parents working.

Maggie came tearing down the hill, just as Serif hopped off the bus.

"Ellie, hold on a sec," she said. I motioned Tessa and Jerome up the hill, and Serif fell in beside them.

"What?" I asked.

Maggie glanced around, smiled briefly as the rest of the moms drifted away, and leaned towards me. "Did you know that the Mitchell house is for sale?"

I stopped and stared at her. "For sale? Since when?"

"Since yesterday. Viv told me."

Vivian Brewster was the local real estate agent. Just about every house bought or sold in Mt. Abrams was handled out of her office. She and Maggie, I knew, were not just neighbors but good friends. "Yesterday? Are you sure?"

Maggie nodded. "Yes. But get this. She told Doug she needed Lacey's signature on the contract, but he told her that he had been given power of attorney. He showed her paperwork. And there's no mortgage.

Everything was paid off a few months ago."

"When her father died," I muttered.

"Whose father?" Maggie asked.

"Lacey's. Her father died in February. And left a lot of money behind. Five million bucks."

Maggie stopped and stared at me. "Her father died? You mean the one who's supposedly sick in Buffalo?"

"Yes," I said.

"Why would Doug lie?"

I shrugged. "I don't know. Lacey's mother still has a phone listing in Virginia, and when I called it yesterday, I got an answering machine."

We had started walking again, and Maggie poked me in the ribs with her elbow. "You actually called her? What for?"

"I don't know. I guess I wanted to see where she was. She dropped out of sight after Doug and Lacey's wedding."

"Maybe *she's* in Buffalo?"

I shook my head, not convinced. "There's something really odd here. And I think we need to find out what it is."

I had stopped eating real food about five months ago.

Let me take that back. I stopped eating food that tasted good and satisfied my various sweet/salty/spicy urges five months ago. Now, I only ate stuff that was good for me, which is why I did not go out with Tessa and Cait for pizza, although I was sure Cait would have appreciated the moral support. I, quite simply, could not be trusted anywhere that pizza or pasta was served. I had pretty much zero willpower about pizza and pasta.

When Tessa was born, I was forty years old. I also weighed almost two hundred pounds. My second pregnancy was quite different from my first. Not only did I eat for pretty much the entire nine months, I continued to eat the following nine months. Being over forty, I did not expect the baby weight to fall off as easily as it had the first time around, but I really hadn't counted on gaining *more* weight.

My marriage started to fall apart. I lost my job. Tessa was a bit whiney. Cait was a teenager—need I say more? I could often be found wandering up and down the aisles of the Stop and Shop, my cart loaded with frozen Sara Lee banana cream pies and bags of Oreos.

After Marc moved out and I started getting side jobs, I began to feel better about myself. When I finally took a cold, hard look at myself in the mirror, I decided drastic action needed to be taken. I joined a gym and tried different diets, with varying levels of success. Last year, when I could no longer kid myself about "baby weight"—after all, it had been years—I started walking every day with Shelly and Carol. My New Year's resolution was to lose the last thirty pounds.

I was almost there.

I was never going to be a size eight. I don't think I was a size eight *ever*. Not even when I was twelve. But my boobs were once again the only part of my body that noticeably stuck out, and I was happy with that.

So there I was, sitting in my kitchen, eating a cold poached chicken breast with a huge side salad and a single slice of cheddar cheese, when Shelly knocked briefly and came through the door.

She glanced around. "The girls?"

"Cait is going to France. Maybe for a while. She's breaking the news to Tessa over pizza."

Her shoulders slumped. "She's going to France? Oh, Ellie, are you okay?"

I nodded and gulped down some lemon-infused water. "Not really, but I'll cope. What's going on?"

She sat down across from me and folded her hands. "Tell me about Lacey."

I told her. Then I told her about what Maggie said. She looked thoughtful, nodding to herself.

"I saw Maggie earlier, and she told me what was going on, but I wanted to hear it directly from you. So, Lacey inherits millions, pays off her house, gives her husband power of attorney, then disappears?"

"To be honest, she didn't exactly disappear. We just don't know where she is," I said. "And I can't find out who inherited the money." I'd spent most of the afternoon reading through that cozy mystery and had decided, after reading the sixth or seventh red herring the author threw on the page, that there was usually a very innocent explanation to everything.

Shelly tilted her head. "We know that Doug lied. Why would he do that?"

"Maybe he was embarrassed. Or caught off guard. I mean, we don't know him at all, and here I was, in his face, asking questions."

Shelly still looked skeptical. "You asked one perfectly innocent and easy question. Was Lacey all right? If there was an easy or innocent answer, why didn't he give it?"

I got up, gathered my empty paper plate and napkin and threw them in the garbage. "I don't know, Shel, but honestly, what can we do? We don't know them at all. Maybe she goes off by herself all the time."

It was odd that living in such a small community for almost a year the Mitchells managed to remain such a mystery. The boys did not exchange play dates. Lacey had made no close friendships or shared any type of personal information at all. We didn't know her birthday. Or her favorite color. Or where she went every day between nine and noon. No one knew what Doug did all day, aside from putting on a suit and driving off every morning by eight-thirty, often returning quite late.

That was still okay. I mean, not everyone who lived in Mt. Abrams was as open and friendly as Shelly Goodwin or Carol Anderson. Or me.

I looked at Shelly. "So, what do you *think* happened?"

She frowned. "I guess I was hoping for a nice, juicy murder plot."

I laughed. "Where do you think we are, Cabot Cove? Listen, I'm joining the Garden Club to help Lynn fend off the evil Mary Rose. Come with me?"

She sighed. "They meet Thursdays, right? Yes, I suppose. Is this about the pavers?"

"I prefer to think of it as the mission to save the hydrangeas from death by road salt."

She stood up. "How can you support death by road salt? I'm in." She sighed wistfully. "A murder would have been nice."

I laughed again. "Not for Lacey."

She laughed with me. "You're right. When is the Cait thing happening?"

I shrugged. "She's flying over for the interview in June. She'll know by August. If she gets in, it's two years. If not, she'll be working at Pierre's forever."

"No, she's a smart kid. She'll figure something out. See you tomorrow."

She closed the door behind her, and I finished cleaning up my kitchen. When Marc and I remodeled ten years ago, we debated as to whether to try to bring the kitchen back to its original 1875 glory. I spent five minutes researching the Victorian kitchen, then ordered extra-tall cabinets and granite countertops. There's a lot to be said for keeping those important period details, but nobody wants three feet of counter space and a single cabinet for storage. We did find a killer vintage gas stove, complete with cast iron fittings and cute chrome knobs, but that was as authentic as we got.

The girls weren't back yet. That meant there was probably ice cream involved. I glanced down at Boot. "Walk?"

She perked up her ears, and we went out the back door.

After the warm day, the cool evening air surprised me. May was a fickle month in New Jersey, tempting you with sunshine then reminding you that snow before Mother's Day was not unheard of. I walked quickly towards the lake. About five minutes of this was all I was going to be able to take.

The Mitchell house was ahead of me. I headed towards it. The porch light was on, and there were a few interior lights on. I slowed as I got nearer. Was it possible to just take a peek inside?

I stopped myself. What was I doing? I may have been curious about Lacey, but not enough to turn me in to a Peeping Tom. Boot caught the scent of something and took off, pulling me up the Mitchell's driveway, past the wraparound porch to the detached garage in back.

The garage had been built later, of course, probably in the forties, and it had two doors that still opened manually, just like my garage. One of the doors was standing open, and I could see Doug's Camry parked between rakes hung on the interior wall and a row of garbage cans. Boot was heading straight for Doug's car until a small dark shape appeared out of nowhere and shot past us. Boot reversed suddenly, spinning me around and practically pulling my arm off.

As I turned, I got a glimpse of the garage interior. Something struck me as odd.

I jerked at Boot's leash and moved closer. I glanced at the house. The last thing I needed was Doug coming out and finding me prowling through his garbage cans and gardening tools.

I skirted the Camry and stopped.

There was a great big nothing where Lacey's Suburban should have been.

Doug said he'd driven her to the train.

I backed out slowly and turned again to look at the house.

If he had driven her, why was her car gone?

That made two lies. In barely three sentences.

Doug was starting to look a bit dicey.

CHAPTER THREE

WHEN THE GIRLS came home, Tessa was not happy. She stood in the middle of the living room, arms crossed defiantly, chin down, pouting. She was a mini-me, the same dark, curly hair, big brown eyes, and thick, straight brows. She was built like me too, skinny legs, narrow hips, and sturdy around the middle. There was always a chance she would grow into a long-waisted nymph like Cait, but I doubted it. My prediction was that she'd be carrying around a fireplug body just like mine for the rest of her life.

"I don't think Cait should go anywhere," she said with conviction. "She won't like it in France. She likes it here."

I pasted on a smile. "Tessa, this is a great chance for Cait to live someplace new and really cool, meet lots of amazing people, and she can work at what she loves."

Tessa glared. "Well, I hope they don't pick her. I hope they like somebody else better."

I put on my stern face. "Tessa, that's being mean. This is something your sister really wants. We should support her and hope for the best."

"Daddy won't let her go."

I glanced up at Cait, who stood behind her sister and rolled her eyes. "Daddy would never keep your sister from doing something she really wanted," I said.

Tessa was not giving up. "When I see him tomorrow, I'm going to tell him, and he'll make Cait stay home."

I sighed. Poor Tessa. Poor Cait.

Actually, poor Marc. He really was a good dad, spending lots of time with Tessa, even taking her on vacation with him to his family's cabin in Maine every summer. His relationship with Cait was different, of course. Father-daughter things were difficult under the best of circumstances, and there was a lot of baggage they were still filtering through. Cait loved her father and spent time with him. She understood that although Marc had been the one to leave, every marriage—and divorce—was about two people.

"Maybe Cait can go with you and Daddy tomorrow. What do you think, Cait?"

Cait rolled her eyes again. "I'll tell Dad about France, and we can all talk about it together, okay?"

Tessa sniffed. "He won't let her go," she said again, then turned and marched out and up the stairs.

I looked sympathetically at Cait. "So, I guess this was not a fun girl's night?"

Cait threw herself into a chair. "How can one little kid be so smart? She came up with three really good arguments for me staying before she went into her *because I said so* mode."

"Well, let's face it, you both had exceptionally brilliant parents. I'd talk to your father tonight and let him know what's going on. If he gets blindsided by Tessa, he won't be happy."

She nodded. "Yeah, you're right." She was quiet. I picked up my book and started reading again.

"What if they don't pick me?" she asked finally, in a very small voice.

I looked over at her. "Baby, they would be complete fools not to pick you. You're a

Renaissance woman, for God's sakes. You speak, what, three languages besides English, you're a literature wiz who's also a science geek, and you can talk the leaves off a tree. How could they not jump at the chance to have you on their team?"

She smiled crookedly. "Thanks, Mom." She pulled herself up and went upstairs.

I tried to get back into my book, but couldn't concentrate. Even though I read books every day for a living, I always chose reading over television at night to relax.

I closed my book and started turning off the lights. I looked out the window and over to the Mitchell house. The porch light was off. The first floor was dark. A blue flicker in an upstairs window told me that someone was watching television. Was it Doug?

No, it wasn't, because there was a light on in the next window, and a tall shadow crossed it. Again. And then again.

Someone was pacing back and forth.

I watched for ten minutes. What was I expecting? That Doug Mitchell would race down the stairs, across the street, and down the road to my front door, where he would tearfully confess that Lacey was stashed in the basement behind the old coal bin?

I shook myself, turned and went upstairs.

It was not unusual for my mother to call me at seven in the morning. In fact, it was typical. She knew I worked during the day, afternoons were usually spent with Tessa, then came dinner. Since my mother was usually asleep by eight-thirty, mornings were her best time. It wasn't *my* best time, but for Mom, I didn't have to be a shining star.

After my father died, Mom sold the house and moved into an assisted living facility. It made sense. We had already been joking about her faulty memory before Dad became sick. I think he convinced her, in those last awful days, that trying to live alone in a three-bedroom, two-story colonial on half an acre was too much for her. I had felt a momentary cringe at the thought of my childhood home being taken from me, but my younger brother, Ted, finished it for me when he drew me aside after the funeral.

"Listen, Ellie, I'm in Chicago," he said. "I can't help out here. Do you want to be the one running every time Mom can't find the remote?"

Mom had a large room in a very nice facility where they sang Broadway show tunes around a grand piano in the lobby every evening after dinner. They also organized weekly trips to Walmart and monthly excursions to museums, local theater, and craft shows. My mother loved her new life. No cooking, no cleaning, and someone else to drive her around.

I had to admit, I was a little jealous.

So when the phone rang in my house at seven-oh-five, I always knew who it was, even without caller ID.

"Hey, Mom, how are you feeling?" I always led with that question, so we could get the complaining portion of the conversation out of the way early.

"Well, you know, my knee." Ah yes, the knee. Cait jokingly referred to it as a "sports injury," as Mom got it when she fell trying to wrestle a Le Creuset Dutch oven marked down to only $150.00 from another equally determined customer at T.J.Maxx.

"Don't take too much Tylenol, Mom."

"Why, it might kill me?" I could picture my mother on her phone. She did not have a cell phone. The technological sophistication had proved too much for her very early in the game. She had a landline in her apartment and a very simple answering machine, and if she felt cheated of the latest marvels of Android and Apple, she didn't show it.

She had a phone chair. It was the same phone chair she'd had in the old house, as well as the same phone table. When she was on the phone, she did not watch television, eat, or do her beloved crossword puzzles. She was all about the phone call. She would sit upright, both hands gripping the phone, eyes closed in complete concentration.

"A little gas last night," she said and sighed. "I don't know why I eat broccoli."

I poured myself some coffee. I had always managed to combine phone conversations with other activities. "High in antioxidants, Mom."

"High in fiber. Mr. Milano almost blasted us out of bingo. What are we doing for Mother's Day?"

"I thought I'd pick you up early; we could have brunch here, then go to the Arboretum. They're having an orchid show."

"I killed the last one I bought," she said sadly.

"I know. You don't have to buy one. We can just look."

"That sounds nice. I hope my knee is better by then."

"It's a few days away, Mom. No tennis and you should be fine."

"You're not funny." She sniffed. "How are my darlings?"

"Caitlyn has a chance to go to France. We're all very excited."

"They don't like us there," Mom pointed out. "And there are bombs."

"Mom, there are bombs everywhere."

"They killed all those poor journalists."

I sipped my coffee, thinking fast. "Mom, she won't be in the journalism district."

"Oh?"

"She'll be in the literature district. Nobody gets bombed there."

"Oh. Well then, that's fine. Maybe Ted can fly out?"

Sometimes I shifted gears as quickly as Mom, and sometimes it took me a bit longer. After trying to picture Ted in the literature district, I took three steps back in the conversation. "You mean fly here for Mother's Day? I'll ask him. He and Calvin would love the orchids."

"Why, is that a gay thing?"

My mother had a bit of difficulty with my brother coming out. She'd been raised in a strict Catholic Italian household, where homosexuality meant an immediate ticket to hell. She became gradually tolerant, even as her grasp on reality began to waver, so the ingrained mistruths of her childhood often became fuddled.

"No, Mom, it's not a gay thing. It's a cool and beautiful thing." Boot came and put her paw on my thigh. She seemed to know when Mom was on the phone and always offered moral support. "When is Walmart day?"

"Tomorrow. I need sunglasses. That damn Justine Caldwell keeps stealing mine."

"Are you sure you aren't misplacing them?" My mother was robbed of some personal belonging at least twice a month, and Justine was the usual culprit. Having met Justine, I doubted her guilt, as the poor woman was confined to a wheelchair and couldn't steal a cotton ball without upping her oxygen intake.

"No. She took them. I wish I had enough money to buy a nice pair."

"Mom, I told you, you have plenty of money. Just ask the aide. You have a spending account, remember?"

"I think Justine stole it."

Boot whimpered and wagged her stub of a tail. "Mom, I've got to go. I'll see you Friday."

"Okay, dear. Give my love to Marc."

That was always the saddest part. Even though Marc and I divorced before she started forgetting things, she had decided in her heart of hearts we were still married, and I'd long ago given up trying to talk her out of it.

Tessa came into the kitchen, face wrinkled with sleep. "Why does Grandma always call so early?"

"Because she knows that I'm usually not doing anything too important, and I can talk to her."

"Can I have some breakfast?"

"Of course. Cereal? Toast? One perfect scrambled egg?"

She slumped into her chair. "Cheerios. Do we have strawberries?"

"Yes. Coffee with that? A side of fries?"

She put her head between her hands in mock despair. "Mom, I'm not treating you like a waitress. I'm not tall enough to reach the cabinet yet!"

"Well, okay. Start growing. It's time you started earning your keep around here. Do a few chores, lift that bale, tote that hay."

She looked at me between her splayed fingers. "Is that a movie thing I never heard of or a Broadway thing?"

I poured her cereal in a bowl and grabbed the milk and berries out of the fridge. "Both. I think we have to start your classical movie education."

She groaned. "No, Mom, please."

"Cait loved classical movie nights."

She chewed. "Yeah, well, Cait's weird." She swallowed. "Did you know that Jordan's grandpa got killed?"

I tried to look completely casual. "Jordan Mitchell? No, I didn't know."

"Well, yesterday I tried to tell him I was sorry his grandpa was sick, and that my grandma sometimes didn't even know who I was, and he got really angry. He said his grandpa got killed."

I swallowed my coffee very carefully. "Really? He must have been very upset."

"He was. Mrs. Winship took him to the nurse because he started to cry. I felt kinda bad."

"Well, baby, it wasn't your fault. You were trying to be kind."

She shrugged and finished her cereal in silence. Then she went upstairs and left me with Boot. I looked down at her soft brown eyes, then I stood up and looked out the window at the Mitchell house.

What the heck was going on there? Where was Lacey Mitchell?

"I think you're being ridiculous," Carol said. We were done with all the hills, and were on the walking path around the lake. This was my favorite part of our walk, through the tall oaks that rimmed the water. Since the path was maintained by the county, the walking trail was wide and well tended, no ruts or sizable rocks to contend with.

"I think the whole thing stinks," Shelly said.

"Maybe," Maggie said. "But what can we do about it?"

"I was thinking about talking to the police," I said.

"And tell them what?" Carol asked.

I had no answer. I'd been running stuff over in my mind, and I had no idea what I thought, let alone what to do.

"Last night, you were convinced we were all overreacting," Shelly said. "Now you want to call the police? What happened?"

"Doug spent most of the night pacing around his bedroom."

Shelly raised an eyebrow. "And we know that how?"

I made a face. "I couldn't sleep. Every time I got up, the light was on, and I could see him pacing."

"Still," Carol said. "That means nothing."

"This morning Tessa told me that she tried to talk to Jordan about the sick grandpa, and Jordan got upset and said *his* grandpa got killed." I looked around. "And I just happened to be walking Boot past the Mitchell house last night, and she was following something into the garage, and the one door happened to be open, and I saw that Lacey's car was missing."

"Grandpa got killed?" Maggie echoed.

"Lacey's car is missing?" Carol asked. "Now that sounds like something."

"Let's look at this," I said. "Lacey's father died suddenly, or was possibly killed, and left a lot of money to someone, maybe Lacey, because for some reason the wife wasn't even mentioned in the obituary. At all. Lacey is gone, and her husband lied about her whereabouts. Her car is gone. And he told us he took her to the train station. We heard him say that.

Her sons are really upset about something."

"You might have something," Carol said slowly. "It's starting to get more complicated. Maybe you could just, you know, talk to a detective or something? In fact, you could go and see Sam Kinali."

"Who?" I asked.

She carefully stepped over a stray tree branch. "He's a detective with Lawrence Township. I've met him a few times. He presented a few programs at the main library, and he seemed very friendly. In fact, I'm closing today and don't have to be a work until four, so I'll go with you."

Going to the police. So, we were going to find out what had happened to Lacey and become neighborhood heroes, or we'd discover that nothing had happened at all and become neighborhood laughingstocks.

We walked a little farther, and Carol spoke again.

"So, I met someone on Fish."

Carol had started dating. Her husband had been dead for almost five years, and recently she'd decided to sign up for every dating site she could find. Her conversations were peppered these days with a sort of cyber-dating shorthand— Fish, JDate, FOB and SOH. Fish was

Plenty of Fish, a dating site, as was JDate. FWB meant friends with benefits (a big no-no for Carol), and SOH meant sense of humor (a must-have).

"Leon. He's age appropriate and financially secure. He wants to meet for coffee."

"Excellent," Shelly said.

"I think so." Carol was the type of woman who still wrote thank-you notes and used linen napkins when she had us all over for lunch. She approached dating with the same efficient sensibility that she used for changing her seasonal house decorations, sending out Christmas cards, and having her tires rotated. For her, there was a proper time and place for everything. Right now, Leon fit in perfectly.

"Does he have a friend for Ellie?" Shelly asked.

"Ellie," I said loudly, "doesn't need his friend."

"Yes, you do," Maggie said. "Do you want to grow old alone?"

I slowed to give Boot the chance to pee all over a fallen log. "I have children, Maggie. I'm never going to be alone."

"Okay, then," she countered. "Do you want Cait choosing your nursing home?"

What could I say to these women? Sure, they were all my friends, and yes, I'd throw myself in front of a bus for them. But I could never admit, not even to these best of confidants that I was still madly in love with my ex-husband.

"I'm sure Cait will do an excellent job, but thanks for thinking of me."

We walked the rest of the way in silence. We all liked to talk, but we all also enjoyed that moment, halfway around the lake, when the only thing you could hear was birdsong and the sound of our breathing.

It appeared that any Lacey Mitchell conversation was closed until we found ourselves directly in front of the Mitchell house. We all stopped and stared.

"I wonder if her car is still gone," Shelly asked no one in particular.

"Are you thinking that someone returned it in the middle of the night?" Carol asked.

We all walked up the driveway. The left-side door of the garage was open, as it always was during the day. Yes, I suppose anyone could have snuck in and stolen any number of empty garbage cans or rakes or shovels, but that usually wasn't a problem in Mt. Abrams.

We walked into the garage. No Suburban.

We started back down the drive, when Shelly stopped short. "The back door is open," she said.

We looked. Yes. The screen was shut tight, but the actual door stood ajar.

"I wonder if somebody's in there," Maggie said in a somewhat hushed voice.

Shelly climbed the back steps, opened the screen, and yelled, "Hello."

Silence.

Shelly opened the door further and yelled again.

"What are you doing?" Carol hissed.

"Checking to see if everything is all right," Shelly said.

"What are you hoping to find?" I called softly.

She turned and grinned. "Who knows? But don't you really want to see what the inside looks like?"

Maggie bounded up the back steps. "Right with you."

Carol cleared her throat. "I refuse to participate in breaking and entering."

"That's fine. Then hold the dogs and yell if somebody comes." I handed her Boot's and Buster's leashes.

She glared at me. "This is actually illegal," she warned.

I climbed the steps behind Maggie and went into the Mitchell house.

"It's very clean." Maggie whispered.

"Why are you whispering?" Shelly asked. "No one is here, remember?"

"What if Lacey is tied up in the attic?" Maggie said, voice still hushed.

"Then she'd probably want to hear another voice so she can stomp on the floor and get rescued," I said. "Do you hear her pounding on the attic floor with her tied-up feet?" We all stopped and stared up at the ceiling. Nothing.

"Okay, then," Maggie said in her normal voice. "It's really clean."

It was. The kitchen had been redone in that pseudo-country style, with whitewashed cabinets, a farmer's sink, and butcher block on the large island. We walked slowly through the kitchen into the dining room, then into the living room, turned left through the hall to a small office, then back into the hall to the stairs.

"And it's pretty," Shelly said.

She was right. The rooms were beautifully decorated, but showed no personality at all. There were no framed photos, no kid art on the side of the refrigerator. The pillows had obviously never been used to smack a younger brother, and nobody had dared to kick at the rungs of the dining room chairs.

It was very quiet. I could hear a clock ticking somewhere, but that was all. All the windows were shut, and the air had a faint potpourri scent. "It's really quiet," I said. My house was always talking to me—a creak of the floorboards, the wind through an off-center window frame, the rustling of leaves against the side of the house.

"With two boys, how is this so clean?" Maggie asked. "Where are all the toys?"

"They must have a maid," Shelly said.

"Maybe they're waiting for *Country Living* magazine to come by for a photo shoot," I said. I put my hand on the stairway banister and looked up the stairway. "What do you think?"

"Well, in for a penny, in for a pound," Maggie said, pushing me up the stairs.

The landing was big enough to function as the family room, and it looked like people lived there. The remote control was on the floor, and video games were crammed into a very large, and I knew, expensive Longaberger basket.

"I'll take the master," Shelly called. "You guys take the boys' rooms."

I stared after her. "Since when did we become Charlie's Angels?" I muttered. Maggie giggled and slipped into a bedroom.

I walked into Jordan's room. I'd like to say I used a clever detecting technique to figure out whose room it was, but since his name was spelled out on the wall in large wooden letters, I couldn't boast too much. His bed was made. All his Legos were in bins, his completed sets on a shelf. There were lots of age-appropriate books on his nightstand and a very scruffy stuffed panda on the bed.

"Guys, come here," Shelly called.

I went back out and followed Maggie into the master bedroom.

Shelly stood in front of the walk-in closet. A walk-in? In Mt. Abrams? Most of the old Victorians had a single closet for the whole family. A walk-in was unheard of.

"Wow," Maggie said reverently. "Look at all that space."

I looked. She was right. There was a lot of room in the closet, because it was half empty. Only men's clothes hung there.

"Her clothes are all gone," Maggie said.

I turned and looked around. There was nothing on the vanity, no perfume bottles, not even a comb. I crossed the room to start opening dresser drawers. They were all empty until I came to one filled with men's socks.

"Nobody packs everything they own just to take a trip, no matter how long they think they'll be gone." I said, closing the last drawer slowly.

"Where did all her clothes go, if she didn't pack them in her car and drive away?" Shelly asked.

Maggie shuddered. "Let's get out of here. This place is too perfect. It's giving me the creeps."

As I stepped back into the landing, I looked up and saw the attic access panel. I stopped so short that Shelly bumped me from behind.

"What?" she asked, then followed my stare. "Do you think?"

I shrugged and reached up, grabbing the chain, and pulling open the attic steps.

My house had the same access. I unfolded the ladder, and we all looked up into the darkness.

"I went up the stairs first," I said. "Somebody else can climb up there first."

Maggie took a deep breath and climbed up the ladder.

I guess I was expecting her to scream in horror, or at least gasp. What she did is laugh and come back down the steps.

"Cleanest attic I have ever seen," she said, refolding the ladder and pushing it back up. "Neatly arranged file boxes and an empty clothing rack. Totally boring."

We went back downstairs and out the back door. Carol was sitting on the picnic table bench, a dog leash in each hand, and a disgusted expression on her face.

"Done? What were you all thinking, just going into that man's house like that? You should all be ashamed of yourselves. And I bet you didn't learn a thing."

I took Boot's leash and shook my head. "Wrong there. We did learn something. Lacey doesn't live here anymore."

Chapter Four

We were in my kitchen, drinking coffee, not talking. I had three projects waiting for me upstairs, and I wouldn't get paid this week if I didn't finish them, but all I could think about was the empty dresser drawers in the Mitchell house.

Shelly had spooned sugar into her coffee and was still stirring it, and the spoon was making soft clinking noises as it hit the sides of the mug. I had been listening to it for what seemed to be ten minutes.

"Shel, stop stirring," I growled. "I think your sugar has dissolved by now."

She shot me a look. "What's with you anyway? You're a bit touchy."

"I think something awful happened to Lacey," I blurted out. "I can't stop thinking about her. Which is so weird, because I don't know her well and certainly don't like her very much. Carol, do you have a number for this Sam person?"

She shook her head. "No, but I can get one. I'll see if we can get an appointment later this morning." She pushed away from the table, got up, and put her mug in the sink. "Shelly, all her clothes were really gone? How very distressing. And before Mother's Day. Poor Lacey. And her poor little boys."

I could hear Cait on the stairs, and she came into the kitchen wearing a T-shirt and a thong. She froze, looked around, then glared at me.

"Gee, Mom, thanks for the warning."

I waved a hand. "Why are you worried? Shelly used to see you naked. So did Carol. You usually aren't up this early."

"Yeah, I know. It's weird. Hey, everyone, just comin' by for coffee." She waved and popped a pod in the Keurig. "Are you having a meeting or something? You look pretty serious."

"We're going to the police about Lacey Mitchell," I told her.

She nodded. "Wow. Well. Are you going to take it to Missing Persons?"

Carol shook her head. "No, dear, I know a detective there. Sam Kinali. Your mother told me about France. How very exciting for you."

Caitlyn actually blushed. Cait grew up loving words, and for her, the library was almost sacred, which put Carol on some sort of pedestal from which she would never be able to climb down. "Thanks, Mrs. B. Yeah, I'm pretty stoked. You make sure Mom doesn't go too crazy."

Carol smiled graciously and left. Shelly sat back and stared at Cait. "Are you sure this isn't about some boy?"

Cait looked at her in surprise. "Boy? You mean like go all the way to France just to be with some guy?"

Shelly shrugged. "Or to go all the way to France to *not* be with some guy."

My daughter turned beet red as she added cream to her coffee mug.

"Cait?" I stared at her, then at Shelly. "Who?"

"It's nothing," Cait muttered and practically ran from the kitchen.

I pushed my coffee away from me and glared at Shelly. "What do you know that I don't?"

Shelly looked very innocent. "Kyle Lieberman."

I frowned. "You mean Kyle Lieberman who was her best friend in third grade?

Skinny Kyle with the awful nose and big blue eyes?"

Shelly was smirking. "Yep. Only his nose isn't awful any more, and his eyes are still as blue. Just graduated from Wharton. MBA. He's been coming home to pack up his things from his parents' house, and I know for a fact he and Cait were seen together down at Zeke's."

Zeke's was Ezekiel's Tavern, an old-style pub right next to the train station, with craft beers on tap and the best burgers in the county. It was a favorite of just about everyone in Mt. Abrams, not just for the food, but also because of its location.

I hardened my gaze at Shelly. "And you didn't tell me because?"

"I just heard last night. Honestly. I would have said something this morning, but the conversation got hijacked."

"Was that the guy in the beemer?" Maggie asked. She lived behind the Lieberman's house. "He was way cute."

My daughter and Kyle Lieberman. Cait, who according to our brief and infrequent conversations on the subject, had spent the last few years going from one casual hook up to another, was perhaps finally finding happiness with the boy almost next door.

Talk about the world being full of mysteries.

Lawrence Township may sound small and country-like, but it was in fact, a very large, sprawling town of over fifty thousand people in an area of over twenty-five square miles, thirty minutes due west of New York City. The police station had been rebuilt about ten years ago, and it was a large, imposing place adjacent to the municipal court right across the courtyard from Town Hall.

Carol and I walked through the glass doors into a small lobby, past the bulletin board to a thick window. A very young-looking officer behind the glass leaned forward to speak into a microphone.

"Yes?"

"I have an appointment with Detective Kinali," Carol said.

The officer nodded, spoke into a phone, and a few seconds later, the door clicked and swung open.

"Come on through," he said.

We walked through the door into a short empty corridor. A door on the other end opened and a man stood there, smiling.

"Mrs. Anderson. How lovely to see you," he said, and we followed him into the squad room.

There were a dozen or so desks, half of them empty, and a buzz in the room, but there didn't seem to be much actually happening. No jaded hookers slumped in a chair, no shivering junkies, not even a happy drunk. Crime in Lawrence Township appeared to be nonexistent. Detective Kinali led us to a small glass-enclosed room, held the door open, then closed it behind us and sat across the small metal table from us. He took out a small notebook and asked us for our names, spelled out, please, then our addresses and phone numbers. He closed his notebook and folded his hands in front of him. "Now, what can I do for you?"

I almost said "marry me." He was pretty much the sexiest man I had ever seen in real life, and I think my tongue was hanging down to the floor.

He was big. Not just tall, although he was probably over six feet, but big everywhere—broad shoulders and a barrel chest, thick neck and large, strong-looking hands. He was probably my age, maybe older, his hair turning silver, with a slight softening at the jaw.

And he looked...dangerous. He was dark skinned, probably Middle Eastern, with dark eyes and thick but beautifully formed eyebrows. There was an energy about him, as though he was ready to spring into action, but it wasn't a nervous kind of energy. Every movement he made seemed deliberate and necessary. His teeth were very white, and his hair was that shiny, almost slick kind of gray that made women want to run their hands through it just to see if it felt as thick and soft as it looked. He didn't have a mustache, but he should have.

"Detective, thank you so much for seeing us," Carol said. "This is my neighbor, Elizabeth Rocca, and she and I have a problem, and we need some professional advice."

He nodded encouragingly. I swallowed hard, but my mouth was so dry I almost choked.

Carol glanced at me. "Ellie?"

What, me? I was supposed to talk? About what? I had looked into Detective Kinali's eyes and completely forgotten why I was here.

"Ellie," she said, a bit more strongly. I tore my eyes from his face and looked at her. Carol. Oh—that's right. We were here because of Lacey Mitchell.

I turned back to Detective Kinali. "We believe something has happened to another neighbor of ours," I said. "We haven't seen her for a couple of days, and there are, well, circumstances."

He raised an eyebrow. "What kind of circumstances?"

I had a brief flash of this man dressed in robes, riding an Arabian stallion through the desert, sword held aloft, like a character from *Lawrence of Arabia*. "Her name is Lacey Mitchell, and she lived with her husband and sons in Mt. Abrams, and no one has seen her since last Friday when she picked up her boys at the bus stop. Her husband says she's with her sick father in Buffalo, but he's lying."

He frowned. "Is he?"

"Yes. Her father died this past winter. Down in Virginia. Suddenly. Apparently, there was a lot of money involved. Millions. And there's a wife, but she wasn't mentioned in the obituary, which I find highly suggestive."

"Of what?"

"Of some sort of separation or divorce, meaning that Lacey would have gotten all the money."

He sat back. "And you know this how?"

I settled myself more squarely in my chair. "I looked it up. I found the marriage announcement, online of course, got Lacey's maiden name, and started looking for the parents. There was an obituary for the father and a small article about all the money. And the mother? Still has a phone in Fairfax, even though she didn't answer, and there's no trace of her online since 2002."

His mouth twitched. His lips were very full and soft looking. "Very enterprising of you, Mrs. Rocca."

"I'm not Mrs. Rocca," I said. "I used to be Mrs. Symons, but not anymore. Now I'm Miss Rocca. Ms. Rocca. Ellie."

"Ellie, then. You must be a very accomplished researcher."

I nodded. "I'm an editor. Freelance. I often have to do fact checking for my clients."

He tilted his head. "Really? Lucky you, spending all your time reading. Although, I imagine you have to read a lot of things that are not to your taste."

I rolled my eyes. "You have no idea. I'm almost done with this mystery and let me tell you, these characters are deaf, dumb, and blind. I figured out whodunit by the second chapter."

He threw back his head and laughed. His voice was so deep that he sounded like his laughter came from the bottom of a well. "If I ever write a book, I'll be sure you read it first. I wouldn't want *my* characters to be thought of so badly." Our eyes met.

Can I tell you? They were the softest, gentlest, most beautiful eyes I had ever seen. And they were smiling at me. The lines around them crinkled, and there was a warmth and spark to them that made my blood pound.

This was ridiculous. I didn't even know this man. How could I think he would be just perfect for me?

"I'm sure there's more," he said.

I leaned forward. "Her ten-year-old told my ten-year-old that his grandpa was killed." I sat back, feeling rather smug. Now that was a tasty piece of information.

"I'm completely unfamiliar with ten-year-old children. Can they be inclined to exaggerate?"

I shook my head. "Not my ten-year-old. So, you have no children?"

He lifted his shoulders, then dropped them. "No. It's better, perhaps. This job is not very family friendly."

"Are you married?" What? What did I just ask him?

He shook his head. "Like yourself, not anymore."

I leaned forward again. "Where are you from? There's a slight accent, but I can't place it."

Beside me, Carol shifted in her chair. I didn't care. I just wanted him to keep on talking.

"My family is from Turkey. I came to this country as a small child, and grew up in Queens. After law school, I went with the NYPD. Five years ago, I decided to look for a less, well, stressful position."

I grinned. "I bet Lawrence filled that bill. Nothing much going on here besides stolen BMWs and rich kids getting drunk. Bor-ing."

He laughed again. "Believe it or not, life out here in suburbia is much more interesting than you'd imagine. In fact, I am constantly surprised at the beautiful and amazing things I come across every day."

He was looking at me. Yes, that's right. At me. And I didn't even blush.

"And now, the possibility of a missing housewife and mother," he said, after a moment. "Is there anything else?"

"Well, her car and all her clothes are gone," I told him. "And the house was just put on the market, and the realtor says Doug, that's the husband, had a power of attorney, and the mortgage was paid off in full a few months ago."

He raised his eyebrows. "You know, realtors don't usually give out that kind of information."

Carol cleared her throat. "That's generally true, detective, but Mt. Abrams is a very...well, close-knit community. The local realtor is a close friend of a friend, and that particular bit of information came to us—how can I put this?—on the sly."

Why wasn't he taking notes? He should have been scribbling madly in a moleskin notebook. Instead, he was sitting there, looking handsome and slightly mysterious and powerful and masterful and...wait. Let me just stop there.

He smiled and folded his hands on the top of the table. "May I ask you a few questions?"

I nodded. Of course he could. No, I wasn't seeing anybody. Yes, I loved walking in the woods and watching sunsets. Yes, I *did* like Italian food, and I'd love to have dinner with him this Friday...

"How do you know that all of Mrs. Mitchell's clothes were gone?"

Of course, he'd have to start with *that* question. I opened my mouth, but nothing came out.

He shifted his gaze to Carol. "I would hate to think," he said softly, "that curiosity caused someone to do something illegal."

Carol leaned forward. "Detective, I swear to you, I did NOT do anything illegal. That particular bit of information didn't even come from Ellie. It came from another source."

Carol managed to tell the absolute truth. Amazing.

He unfolded his hands and placed them, palms down, on the table. "Before I do anything official," he said, "I'll call down to Virginia and see if anything was suspicious about the father's death. I'll also see if we can find a plane ticket issued to Mrs. Mitchell in the last few days. There are all sorts of perfectly reasonable explanations for what is going on. The first thing that comes to mind is that she packed up her belongings and left her husband. Most of our missing persons have usually run away on their own."

Boy, did I feel like an idiot. Lacey left home. She took her five million bucks and just left. So much for my brilliant powers of deduction, honed by years of editing mystery novels. She left; he was embarrassed by it, and since the children don't know yet, he'd made up an innocent lie

Poor Doug. I glanced over at Carol and could tell she was thinking the same thing.

Detective Kinali smiled graciously. "Nevertheless, this is certainly interesting. Thank you, ladies." He stood. "Thank you for coming in."

He gestured towards the doorway, and Carol and I filed neatly out.

We were walking to the exit, and I felt like my head was going to explode. Lacey left Doug. Of course she did. And I had to go make a fool of myself in front of such an attractive man. I caught my breath. Where did this come from? I still had fantasies getting back together with Marc, yet, and here I was, practically paralyzed with what — lust, love, need, want? I remembered when I was sixteen years old, and Bobby McGowan walked into art class. I fell immediately in love. That's exactly how I felt, only, you know, with thirtysomething years of wisdom and experience telling me how crazy it all was. But—whatever it was, I could not ignore it.

I came to a full stop. "Hold on, Carol. Was it just me, or was there something going on between Detective Kinali and myself?"

She sighed. "Really? You have to ask? Good Lord, there were sparks flying across the table." She lifted her eyebrows and tightened her lips. "I half expected you to sit back and light a cigarette."

"I'll be right back." I turned to march back towards Detective Kinali.

Let me put this out there right now— I'm not brave. I don't take lots of chances. I'm also not very impulsive. So I cannot explain why I went back to his desk and sat down abruptly across from him, except that, if I didn't, I'd hate myself for the rest of my life.

He tilted his head and smiled at me. "Is there anything else I can do for you?"

My tongue was frozen to the roof of my mouth. All I could imagine were those strong hands around me. "Yes. Would you like to have a drink with me tomorrow night?"

His smile broadened. "As a matter of fact, yes. Nicola's at eight?"

I nodded, then bolted from the chair and practically ran back to Carol.

I was hyperventilating by the time I burst outside. Carol grabbed my arm and shook me, hard.

"Ellie, what happened? What did you say to him?"

"I asked him out. And he said yes."

She raised an eyebrow. "Good for you. That man is hotter than a witch's tit."

She patted down her hair and walked calmly towards the car.

Yes, he certainly was.

My work was finished. I had done a bit of snooping, satisfied my inner Nancy Drew, then gone to the correct authorities, and now the situation was in the hands of people who actually knew what they were doing and would probably find Lacey hanging around a pool in the Caymans with a studly twenty-three–year-old. So I did not spend the day not working, staring out the window, and thinking about what had happened to Lacey. I spent it not working, staring out the window, and thinking about Detective Sam Kinali.

I'd had this kind of blind, all consuming crush before. After Bobby McGowan set the bar in high school, at least three equally momentous attachments had followed throughout college. It all ended when I met Marcus Symons, three days after I got my first job as a very junior assistant to an assistant in a major publishing house. Right from the start, I knew Marc was different, because I didn't just want to spend all my time with him naked. I also wanted to talk to him. Marc had been the smartest, most interesting person I'd ever been close to, and talking to him became one of my life's real joys.

Now, I wanted to talk to Sam Kinali. I wanted to know if he'd ever been back to Turkey and what it had been like for him growing up in the United States with immigrant parents. Why had he become a cop instead of a lawyer? Why had his marriage failed? What was his favorite food?

I'll be honest and admit that I also wondered what he'd look like without all those clothes, if he'd be hairy—not that I'd mind—how his skin would feel, and if those lips were as soft as they looked. And all that controlled energy—how would *that* translate?

By the time I had to pick up Tessa, I was so hot and bothered I felt like I should take a shower.

"When is Daddy coming?" Tessa asked.

I swung her backpack over my shoulder. "When does Daddy always come?"

"Five-thirty."

"Okay, then. There's your answer."

She raced ahead. Maggie fell in step next to me. "How did it go with the police?"

I glanced around. No one was too close. "We gave all the info, and a detective said he'd check some things out," I told her. "His first thought is that Lacey packed herself up and took a powder."

Maggie made a face. "Yeah, I guess that's just as likely as Doug killing her, then packing up all her things nice and neatly, stashing them in her car, then driving the Suburban into the lake."

"The detective, Sam Kinali, is going to be my new fantasy boyfriend."

Her eyes lit up. "Do tell!"

"He's big and sexy and dangerous-looking, and his eyes are beautiful, and he's Turkish, so I keep imagining us in the middle of the desert somewhere in a big tent, drinking sweet wine and lolling around on pillows." I glanced at her. "I asked him for a drink."

She snorted. "Oh, Ellie, did you switch to editing romance novels? Is that where this is coming from?"

"No. I just finished a tedious mystery with no character development and a plot full of holes. If the author doesn't do a complete rewrite, she doesn't stand a chance of selling a single copy."

Maggie made a face. "Ouch. What happens when you tell a person something like that?"

I shrugged. "If they want to get their money's worth, they'll do what I say. If they want a cheerleader, they'll get another editor. I get paid to be a hard-ass."

She laughed. "And you're such a softie in real life."

I chuckled. "Yeah, well, that's because you don't get paid for real life. See you tomorrow."

I had not seen Cait all day. She yelled good-bye at some point in the morning and did not reappear until just before her father was due to pick her and Tessa up. Kyle Lieberman? I dared not ask.

Marc beeped from the curb, and the two girls tumbled out of the house and into his car. I waved from the porch, then walked over to Shelly's house.

Shelly lived a bit farther down the hill where the houses were still from the late 1800s but were smaller, with even more embellishment. In fact, her whole block looked like a Christmas card in winter, without the snow, of course, a row of gaily painted visions gilded with candles and gingerbread trim. Shelly lived in a long but narrow house with a deep front porch and double glass doors in front. I knocked, then pushed my way in.

Shelly and I had been going in and out of each other's houses for so long that our respective dogs didn't even bark anymore. I went past her sons, sprawled on the couch watching television, and back into the kitchen.

She was standing over the stove, stirring something and muttering to herself. She glanced up, saw me, and grinned. "So, you've hooked a hottie?"

I slumped against the counter and peered into the pot. "Chili? Are you grumpy about chili?"

"I'm not grumpy about the chili. I'm just grumpy in general. They're setting up a new billing system at work, and you know how I am about computers."

I did know. Shelly apparently had a special electromagnetic force surrounding her that invariably infected every electronic device that came into her orbit. She'd been through so many cell phones that I wouldn't even let her borrow mine. The things that happened to her various computers and laptops would have sent all of Silicon Valley into a tailspin.

"Sorry," I said. "And yes, I have a date with a very sexy man, and I haven't dated in twenty-six years. Do you think much has changed?"

"Ask Carol. Then again, don't ask Carol. When I saw her earlier she was trying to decide what color pantyhose to wear to meet Leon. I didn't know anyone wore pantyhose anymore."

"Just Carol. At least I feel better about Lacey. I mean, this detective seemed to take us seriously. I think he'll really find something out, if there's anything *to* find. But I'm pretty sure he's right, and Lacey just...left."

"Yeah, I get having a bunch of money and leaving the old life behind, but her kids? She wasn't exactly the warm and fuzzy type, but I think she really loved those two boys."

I was trying to think. "How was she when she picked them up Friday afternoon? Do you remember? Did she seem like she was extra clingy because she was never going to see them again?"

"I'm not there for pick up, remember? Ask Maggie. As for you, you got a date out of it. Sounds like a good day all round. Marc has the girls, right? Want to stay for chili?"

I shook my head. "No, thanks. Celery and cottage cheese tonight. I have to save calories for tomorrow night in case things get crazy and there's an appetizer with the drinks."

"Well, it's paying off. You look really good. Pre-Tessa good."

I looked down at myself. "Thanks. I was going to fill you in on my day, but as usual, you know more about it than I do." I shot her a look. "What's with Cait and Kyle?"

She grinned. "Doesn't that sound so cute? Cait and Kyle?" She shrugged. "They've been seen down at Zeke's. A couple of times. That's all. Why don't you ask her?"

I shuddered. "Ask my daughter about her love life? Are you kidding? We agreed on Don't Ask Don't Tell when she was sixteen. Well, I'm outta here. See you tomorrow."

I walked back home, ate carrots, cottage cheese, and celery with all-natural peanut butter. I called my brother, inviting him to fly out for the weekend, but he was spending the day with Cal's mother. We talked for a long time. Ted was not just my brother, he was one of my best friends, and we always had lots to share. I finally hung up, and since I had gotten very little work done, I went upstairs and made it a point not to look out my window towards the Mitchell house.

I was in the zone when the girls came home, because I didn't even hear the car or the front door slam. I snapped out of a rather spicy interrogation scene and hurried downstairs at the sound of Tessa's yelling.

I turned into the kitchen and stopped short. Marc was there.

I hadn't been in the same room with him in over six months. When Tessa announced she was old enough to go from house to car door without an escort, Marc and I stopped needing any regular face-to-face interaction. But I knew why he was in my kitchen. Tessa was throwing a fit, and he was trying to calm her down.

He was on his knees in front of her, and she was yelling at him, her little face mere inches from his own. Cait was slumped against the doorjamb, looking miserable.

"Whoa, Tessa, stop yelling," I said, loud enough for her to hear. She turned and ran to me, throwing her arms around my waist.

"Daddy won't make Cait stay home," she wailed, then burst into tears.

Well, damn.

Marc looked up at me miserably. "I don't know what to say," he said over the sound of Tessa sobbing.

Tessa was getting tall and was all gangly arms and legs, but she was still my baby. I picked up my little girl and carried her up to her room.

She took a while to cry it out, but she finally settled into a hiccupping bundle, half on her bed and half in my arms.

"Tessa, honey, you are making us all very sad by acting this way," I said softly. "You're hurting Caitlyn and your Daddy and me. I know you love your sister and don't want her to leave, but this is important to her. And when you love somebody, you can't keep them from following their dreams."

She sniffed. "What about my dreams?"

I stroked her hair. "What are your dreams, baby?"

"That Caitlyn and I live together on a farm with six horses and a goat."

"Oh." I kissed the top of her head. "And when were you going to do that?"

"After I got out of vet school." She sat up and wiped her eyes. "And we were going to have lots of rescue dogs, and I'd take care of them for free."

"That's a great dream, Tessa. But isn't Cait going to have to wait an awfully long time for you to get out of vet school?" She nodded, then looked at me with narrowed eyes. She was a smart kid. She knew where this was going.

"So, while she's waiting," I went on, "shouldn't she be able to do what *she* wants?"

She took a deep breath. "But she'll be gone for two years."

I hugged her. "I know. I'll miss her too. But we can Skype and stuff. She can still text you all the time."

She buried her face in my side. "Not the same."

"I know. But it's what we've got."

She nodded.

"Good. Now go downstairs and say goodnight to Daddy, and then take a quick shower, OK?"

She uncoiled herself and slid off the bed and out the door. I sat there for a few minutes, looking around her room. She was still in the princess stage, the pink and purple stage, the stuffed animal stage. I knew that at any moment I would turn around, and she, too, would be going off on her own into the great unknown.

A few minutes later, Cait and Tessa came back upstairs. I got off the bed and met them in the hall.

"How are my favorite girls now?" I asked.

Cait gave me a hug. "She's a tough bug, but I think we're good." She glared at Tessa, who promptly stuck out her tongue and scurried to the bathroom.

"Dad's still downstairs," Cait said, then went into her room.

I went downstairs slowly. I could hear Marc talking, and I knew he was lecturing Boot. He had been crazy about that dog and would spend evenings lecturing her on various subjects, from proper canine behavior in public to how to properly clean her butt. Cait had especially loved those times, and she would be collapsed in giggles by the time Marc was done.

But tonight he was sitting alone in what used to be his living room, and I could hear him…

"And don't forget to go in everyday and smell Cait's room. You don't want to forget her," he said.

I paused to watch him, sprawled in the corner of the couch, Boot practically on his lap with her ears perked in intense concentration.

"Spend more time with Tessa, until she becomes a pain, then pee on the floor a little so she goes away on her own."

"Please," I said with a grin, "do not telling that dog it is okay to pee in the house."

He looked up and smiled. "I told her just a little."

His smile could still make my stomach do flips. When he left, he had truly broken my heart. It had taken me three years to get over his being gone. I never got over being in love with him. Looking at him now, I could still feel his body against mine. I knew the way his skin tasted, and the sound of his breath in the night.

"How are you?" I asked. It felt easy, standing on the other side of the room.

After not being alone with him for so long, I wasn't sure how I would feel. It wasn't bad.

"I'm good," he said, scratching Boot behind her left ear. "The babe is up and grown."

I nodded. "We'll get used to it, I guess. I'm really happy for her."

"How's your mom?" he asked.

I shrugged. "The same. Maybe worse. I see her every Friday for lunch." I had a sudden flash. "I'm taking her to the orchid show this Sunday for Mother's Day. Would you like to come? She always asks for you."

He smiled. "Sure. Since my own mother still insists on celebrating Mother's Day alone in the Caribbean, I've got nothing else to do."

"Great. I'll let you know the details. The girls will love it."

He was watching me. "You look really good."

I shrugged. "Yes, well, losing fifty pounds will do that."

He shook his head. "Not just that. You look happy."

"I am. Work is good, money's coming in, I've got friends. I've even got a date."

He raised his eyebrows. "A date? Good for you." He glanced around. "You painted the living room?"

"Last year. When Cait was around for Christmas break. We went for gray rather than the usual taupe. I like it"

He got up. He was not tall, barely five foot ten, and was slightly built. His hair was dark red, the color of fall leaves and copper wire tangled together. His eyes were a deep green, his skin fair and freckled. He had aged a bit, a trace of gray at the temples and a tired look around his eyes.

I suddenly thought of Sam Kinali, all big and dark and sexy. I blinked, and there was Marc again, hands in the pockets of his jeans, and he seemed suddenly frail.

"You look tired," I told him.

He shrugged. "Yeah, well, you know publishing. And right now it's even a bigger cluster fuck than ever."

I nodded. "I bet. I'm still in a lot of the loops. Still get *Publisher's Weekly*. Not a pretty picture"

He nodded a few times, looking down at the floor. That meant he was thinking, and thinking hard. "So, a date?"

"Yep. First date in a really long time."

"Well." He looked up. "I still love you, you know that, right?"

I think I stopped breathing. He what? He just said *what*?

I finally exhaled. "Yeah, sure. You're just not *in* love with me anymore, right? Isn't that what you said?"

He walked past me to the front door, turned around, and grabbed me by my shoulders and kissed me.

The feel of his lips on mine was such a shock that I almost fell to the floor. And it wasn't just his lips. I felt his fingers as they gripped my shoulders, and then the slim, hard line of his body pressed against me, and I opened my mouth to him as all sorts of things came crashing in—familiarity, lust, happiness, more lust, that oh-my-God-he-wants-me-back feeling.

I pushed him away and stepped back. "And what the hell was that?"

He looked down at the floor again. "I've missed you," he said at last.

"So? I'm sure you miss your brother out in San Diego. Do you give him a lip lock when you see him too?"

He shook his head. "No, of course not, but—"

"But what? We haven't been in the same room together for months, and you think you can just, well, what you did?"

He looked at me. His eyes were full. Was he crying? "I miss you," he said again. And walked out the door.

I put my hand to my mouth. My lips were still tingling. The rush I had felt had settled down in, well, you-know-where.

He still loved me. He missed me.

Damn him anyway.

CHAPTER FIVE

THE NEXT MORNING it was raining, which suited my mood perfectly. I'd slept very badly the night before, plotting various forms of ecstatic sexual reunion and/or severe mental and physical torture, with Marc as the central figure. Throw in Sam Kinali and his incredibly gorgeous eyes, and it was a pretty disrupted night.

Sometimes, when it rained, I drove Tessa to the bus stop, but today brought a light, warm spring shower, so we put on matching yellow fisherman's slickers and walked down the hill.

Carol and Co. did not walk in the rain. Or the snow, for that matter, or when it was below thirty degrees. Taking Boot for a long walk to make up for the lack of exercise was out of the question. She did not like getting her feet wet. Yes, I know, spaniels are sporting dogs, and you'd think they would be fine in any weather, but—no. Not Boot. She started dragging her feet at the third raindrop. Puddles made her whimper. What a dog.

One of the advantages of the kind of community that was Mt. Abrams was that certain traditions remained intact. Marie Wu, for example, moved into the farmhouse style house across from the bus stop five years ago, and when she was told that her front porch was the spot of the school kids to take shelter during the rain, she just nodded and smiled. So there we were, crowded around Marie's rocking chairs and empty planters, waiting. Shelly was at the opposite end of the porch, so I couldn't fill her in on the latest Marc development, but I knew I'd talk to her later in the day.

The bus came and went, and I started back up the hill. It was raining harder, and I had the hood of my slicker pulled up over my head, so I didn't hear the car as it drove up beside me, not until a voice was calling my name.

"Ellie, how about a lift?" It was Doug Mitchell, his window rolled down, smiling at me.

"Ah…" This was odd. Doug had never said more than five words in a row to me.

Was he really trying to suddenly be a good neighbor? Why? "I'm good."

"Ellie, it's pouring."

It was pouring. What could I say? "Sure. Thanks."

I ran around to the passenger side and jumped in the front seat. I was dripping all over his nice leather interior.

"Oh, Doug, I'm sorry. Everything is getting wet."

He was driving slowly. "No worries. I'm glad I saw you walking. I need to ask you a question."

I was busy with my seat belt. Yes, I was only two minutes away from home, but well, it was a thing. "Sure. What?"

"Why were you in Jordan's room yesterday?"

I opened my mouth. Then I shut it. I swallowed hard. "What are you talking about?" I said, very proud that my voice did not tremble, squeak, or crack. My heart started to beat a little faster. I was a terrible liar. More than that, I was guilty as charged.

"Well, you see, Ellie, when Jordan was little, he kept insisting that someone came in his room at night. So Lacey and I set up a nanny-cam, just to show him that it was only his imagination, you know? These days, I just automatically reset it every night for him. It's a very sophisticated piece of equipment. Motion activated. So imagine my surprise when I looked at the log and saw that the camera went on when no one was supposed to be home."

I stared straight ahead, barely breathing. His voice had started out calmly enough, but he was talking faster and faster, and his tone was changing. He sounded angry. He had a right to be.

I was trying to think a way out of this, but seriously, how could I? Caught on nanny-cam. I thought that sort of thing only happened on reality shows.

"We walk past your house every morning," I told him. When caught, try the truth. My father used to tell me that all the time. "And yesterday, Boot chased a rabbit into your yard, and we followed, and Shelly saw that your back door was open, so we went in to check to see if anything was wrong. It was a good deed sort of thing." Oh, God, that sounded *so* lame.

"I see." His voice was tight. "And you went upstairs because…?"

Very good question, Doug. I stared out the window. We were almost to my house. I could leap out of the car, run inside, lock my door and avoid him for the rest of my life.

"Did she send you?" he whispered hoarsely. "Did she?"

He suddenly sounded afraid. Of what? I turned to him. "Did *who* send me?"

His jaw was clenched, and his hands gripped the steering wheel like it was his last link to the real world. "I didn't think she made any friends, but of course, she'd use you against me." He seemed to be talking to himself more than to me. He was white as a sheet, and sweat had broken out across his forehead. "What did she send you there for?"

"Doug," I said slowly and a little loudly, because, honestly, I was starting to panic. He was freaking out about something. "I don't know what you're talking about."

He jammed on the brakes, put the car into park, and turned in his seat. He looked desperate, and I was suddenly afraid. This was not about me being in Jordan's room. This was a lot more than that.

"What did she tell you?" he asked harshly. "You know she's a liar, don't you?"

I laid my hand slowly on the latch to open the car door. I needed to be away from here. This had gone from embarrassing to scary to something totally beyond scary in just a few heartbeats. I lifted the latch gently, but of course, it was locked. "Doug, who are you talking about?"

He lunged forward, his face suddenly inches from mine. "She got everything she wanted," he screamed at me. "She said she would leave us alone." He had to be talking about Lacey. Why had she left? And why was he so terrified of her coming back?

I was done. My blood was pounding so hard I could feel it trying to burst through my heart and out of my chest. I looked down, found the lock button, pressed it, and pushed the car door open. He grabbed at me, caught my wrist, and twisted. There was a brief spurt of pain, but I jerked my arm, and his fist closed on the sleeve of my rain slicker. I pulled away, leaving him holding the empty slicker, and went running out into the rain and up the street towards my house. I was afraid to look back. He was in a car. He was obviously crazy. What if he tried to run me over?

I swerved off the street and jumped up on the stone wall bordering my yard. I immediately slipped, falling on my face in the wet grass, but at least I was on the other side. He couldn't run me over without plowing through hundred-year-old puddingstone and mortar. I struggled to my feet, soaked, sprinted through to the back yard, and then slowed enough to glance over my shoulder.

Doug's car had not moved. It was still in the middle of the street, wipers on, motor idling, my bright yellow slicker spilling out the open car door.

I ran through the lilac bushes, up the steps, and into the house. I locked the back door with unsteady hands. Then I raced to the front door and threw the dead bolt. I sank to the floor, shaking uncontrollably, breathing in great gulps, Boot whimpering at my side.

I had texted Maggie. I was still huddled on the floor when Boot started barking. Seconds later, there was a pounding on the door behind me.

"Ellie, are you okay?"

I struggled to my feet and unlocked the door. Maggie was standing there, Vivian Brewster behind her. She came in, grabbed my arm, and pushed me back into the kitchen.

"You need tea," she said. I sat down. My breathing was back to normal, but I was drenched and felt cold. I think I was shivering. Viv had been in my house enough times to know my kitchen, and she pulled out mugs and tea bags. Maggie had vanished, but returned with a throw from the living room and put it around my shoulders. I wiped my face with the corner of the throw and pulled it tightly around me.

There was silence, until a mug of tea was put in front of me. I took a grateful sip and closed my eyes.

"Do you want to call the police?" Maggie asked.

I shook my head.

"Ellie, you sent me a text that Doug was after you. Are you sure?"

I took another sip. "Is he still parked out front?"

"No," Viv said.

"He has my slicker." My teeth had stopped chattering.

"We'll get it back," Maggie said. "What happened?"

I told them. I looked into my tea, sipping it as I spoke. When I was done, I looked up at them. "What should I do?"

Viv sat back, folded her arms across her chest, and shook her head. "Girl, you are into *something* here."

Vivian Brewster, besides being a very successful business woman, was the kind of person you wanted in a dire emergency, because she never seemed fazed by events around her. A few years ago, when Hurricane Sandy came through and Mt. Abrams was without power for eight days, she got the key to the Josiah Abrams original summer retreat, which had become the clubhouse for the Lake Association. It still had gas for cooking and a fireplace in every room, and she set up a place where we could all come to get warm and fed.

She was also beautiful, with skin the color of coffee with a hint of cream, high cheekbones and wide dark eyes. She could have easily been taken for an African princess, but when she opened her mouth, Bayonne would come out.

She wagged her finger at me. "Breaking into that house? You both *know* those people aren't right. And now you have him goin' all kinds of crazy on you, and not in a good way." She shook her head again. "What *were* you all thinkin'?"

Just hearing Viv's voice made me feel better. I love Maggie to death, but despite her coolness and bravado, most of the time she tended to be useless in a crisis. Thank God for her husband, because every time

Serif skinned a knee or bumped her head, Maggie would get hysterical while Derek applied first aid. With Viv in my kitchen, I wouldn't have cared if Doug came through the door with a machete.

"I think he was really scared of something," I said, putting down my mug and running my hand through my damp hair. "And who did he mean by *she*? Lacey?"

"I thought you all thought that *he* was the one to be afraid of," Viv said.

"I know," I said. "But who else could he have been talking about?"

We sat in silence. The rain had stopped, and the breeze coming into the house was warm and damp. I was feeling less chilled but needed to get out of my wet clothes.

"I'm fine now. Honestly. I was just, well, panicked," I said.

"I don't blame you. Doug doesn't sound very stable," Maggie said.

I shook my head. "No he wasn't."

"What are you going to do tomorrow morning at the bus stop when you see him? Pretend this never happened?" Viv asked.

I shrugged. "I don't know. I'll figure something out."

But I never had to. When Tessa came off the bus, she told me that Jordan was pulled out of class before lunchtime. The jungle drums sounded quickly, and by the time I was getting ready for my date with Sam Kinali, I got a text from Maggie. She had just left the library and had heard from Carol Anderson that Doug withdrew both boys from school. He told Denise Whitmore, school secretary and Carol's yoga buddy, that he and the boys were going to be staying with Doug's sister, beginning immediately, and for an indefinite amount of time.

Getting ready for a date when you haven't had one since before the existence of the Internet is not nearly as much fun as it sounds, especially when you can't fit into anything that looks even remotely sexy because all the sexy clothes are size ten, and you're not quite there yet. Tessa was of no help, because she didn't think I should be going out at all. Cait viewed the entire operation with ill-concealed amusement.

"It's only a drink, Mom. Or are you expecting something more?"

I tore my eyes from my once-again disappointing image in the mirror and glared at her. "No, I am not expecting anything more. But my generation has a different definition of the word *date*. We don't just accidentally bump into each other and decide to hang out or hook-up or whatever else you Millennials do. We plan ahead and try to make a nice impression."

I pulled off outfit number six, decided a skirt or dress was too fussy anyway, and started hauling out my dress pants. I knew I had black pants from the Gap that I'd bought last winter, but they were actually too big. I found a dark purple tunic I'd had for a couple of years with black embossing around the shoulders and a V-neck, and long flowing sleeves. A little hippy-dippy, but it fell midthigh and hid the fact that the pants were too big and were being held up by a bright green belt.

"You could wear leggings with that," Cait said. She was sprawled on my bed watching. I turned around and looked at myself from the back.

"Women with hips like mine should not be wearing leggings," I muttered. The bulk around my waist was noticeable. Just perfect.

"If you wear them with that shirt, you'll look fine," Cait said.

"I don't own leggings," I told her.

She got off the bed and ran out. I stared at myself unhappily for a few seconds, then undid the pants and let them drop to the floor. I was running out of options as I stepped out of the pants and kicked them to the corner.

Cait came in holding a jumble of black and her cowboy boots. "Here, put these on."

I held up the leggings. "You weigh, like, nothing. These will never fit."

"One size fits all," she insisted.

I sat down and started pulling them on. Yes the leggings were tight, but not uncomfortable. And I could feel where they were packing in all my flabby bits like sausage into a casing. I got up and looked in the mirror again.

"Wow. This might work," I said, surprised.

"Try the boots," she said. Our foot size was the only size we shared. The boots were black with deep gold embellishment, added a few inches to my height, and looked much cooler than I felt.

Cait grinned. "My work here is done. Some gold jewelry, and you'll knock him dead," she said as she walked out.

I looked at myself from the back again. Much better. I found a long gold necklace and some dangly earrings, and decided I looked just fine.

I had told Cait about what had happened with Doug, and although she did not seemed concerned, I did not want my two daughters home alone. On the way out I gave Cait twenty dollars, told her to head to the mall with Tessa, buy something for dinner, and plan on getting home around ten. Tessa's eyes lit up at the prospect of being out so late on a school night, almost distracting her from her disapproval of my date. I kissed them good-bye and drove slowly past the Mitchell house. There were no lights, and the left side of the garage was open and empty. Doug had not returned from wherever he'd taken his sons. Besides, I'd only be gone an hour.

Nicola's was on the other side of Lawrence, a nice Italian bistro with a very comfortable bar and live music on the weekends. I pulled into the parking lot, smoothed my hair, and went inside.

He was waiting for me, which made me smile. He had snagged a booth in the back and was nursing what looked to be a scotch. I slid into the booth and smoothed my hair again. It hadn't rained since the morning, but it was humid, and my hair had a tendency to frizz, even after being doused with Moroccan oil.

"Hi," I said, somewhat breathlessly.

"Hello," he said. "You look lovely." He raised his hand to signal the waitress.

"Thanks," I said. "My daughter is very good at dressing me."

He raised an eyebrow. "The ten-year-old?"

The waitress materialized. "White wine," I said.

She nodded. "Sure. Something to snack on? Would you like to see a menu?"

I would have loved to see a menu and would have probably ordered stuffed potato skins, loaded nachos and fried mac-and-cheese balls.

Luckily, Sam intervened. "Maybe just some spiced almonds, unless you..." he looked over at me, and I shook my head.

"That sounds great," I said to the waitress. She vanished, and I turned my attention back to Sam. "Actually, I also have a twenty-four–year-old. She's the one that contributed to this evening's outfit."

He smiled broadly and nodded. "I see. That must be interesting, two daughters so far apart in age. Are they much alike?"

I shook my head. "Caitlyn, she's the oldest, takes after her father. Redheaded, slender, freckles everywhere. And she's an absolute brain. Tessa looks like me. And she's just your average super-smart kid, which is fine with me. One genius in the family is more than enough."

He drank some scotch. "How long ago were you divorced?"

"Four years. You?"

"Seven." He stopped talking while the waitress set down my wine, then the almonds. "It was hard," he continued. "I did not want my marriage to end. But I could see her point. My job made things very…difficult. Shortly after that, I retired from the force and came out here. Life is much easier for the police here in Lawrence."

I took an almond and nibbled one end. "Speaking of which, did you find anything out? About Lacey Mitchell?"

"Ah," he said. "Yes, I did."

Silence. I sipped some wine. "And?"

"Really now, Ellie, do you think I should be telling you such things?"

"The thing is," I reasoned, "I am the one who came to you, remember? Maybe just a hint?"

He shook his head.

"Oh come on, just one thing, okay? Like, if Doug has ever been, you know, arrested for anything?"

"No, he has never been arrested," Sam said.

I made a face. "Well, I guess since this *is* a date, I'll stop pumping you for information."

He threw back his head and laughed. "Thank you. I'd hate to spend the evening trying to evade your clever and subtle questioning. I'm sure I'd find it exhausting."

I laughed with him. "Yeah, that's me. Clever and subtle."

He looked good. He was wearing a light-weight V-neck sweater over a T-shirt, a look I usually didn't think too much of, but on him…perfect.

"So," he said, "should we spend the next half hour bashing our ex-spouses? I don't have much to say about mine, and I'd much rather talk of other things, but I'll be happy to give you the opportunity." He spoke very carefully.

"Is that how most of your dates start off? Dragging exes through the mud?"

He shrugged. "It happens. Frequently. It seems you women have quite a lot to say about the men in your lives."

I sipped my wine. "That's interesting. I mean, that's what my girlfriends are for. I'd rather spend my time dazzling you with my charm, wit, and boundless sex appeal."

He laughed again. "Excellent. I was hoping you were different. So tell me something else. Did you have a happy childhood?"

"Very. My mom and dad stayed married until he died; my brother and I were very close—still are—and I even had a pony. No trauma, no drama, no secrets. How about you?"

"I was the youngest of six. My parents had no money when they came to this country, just a horde of children and the address of an uncle in Albany. He let us live in his basement until my parents found jobs. Our family's proudest moment was when we moved into our own three-bedroom row house. All of us kids worked; my father had two jobs, and my mother also worked and took care of us all. They never let go of their old ways, but made sure each of their children was one hundred percent American. The name on my original birth certificate is unpronounceable, even to me. My parents changed my name to Sam when they moved here. After Uncle Sam. We became citizens as soon as we could. I loved history, but I was encouraged to study only American history. Turkey's past is long and illustrious, but also filled with much regret." He shrugged. "My father was in the army when he was young. I imagine he did terrible things. That's probably why they left."

I was fascinated. "Did you ever ask them about the past?"

He shrugged. "They wouldn't talk about it, and we never asked. My oldest brother went back to Turkey and lived there for some time, but he eventually returned to the States. If he learned anything while he was there, he never said." He took a long drink. "We were a close and loving family, but there were boundaries. And as children, we learned to respect those boundaries."

I sat back. "It would drive me crazy to think that there was a family history that I didn't know."

He smiled. "It drove me crazy too. It still does. But my parents are still alive, and I will not disrespect them. When they are gone..." he lifted his shoulders, then let them drop. "I am, after all, a detective."

"Have you ever been back to Turkey?"

He shook his head. "One day, I will go. But only when I know that, if I choose, I can stay. I think that once I am there, I will be taken in."

I propped my arm on the table and put my chin in my palm. "Wow."

He raised his eyebrows. "Did you just say wow?"

"Yes. I mean, that's an amazing thing to say. You must know yourself very well."

"Of course. After all, I've lived with myself for a very long time."

"I have too, but I'm still a work in progress. I never know what I'm going to do from one moment to the next." I picked up another almond and examined it closely. "For instance, I never imagined myself asking a man I just met out for a drink."

"Oh? You don't date much?"

"I don't date at all."

He sat back. "Really? But you're an attractive woman. Surely, I'm not the first man in four years to notice?"

I chewed the almond. "Um…ah, well, you see, I work from home, so workplace romance is kind of off the table. Since most of my friends are, you know, married I don't have many opportunities to go trolling for men."

He took it in. "So that is why you don't have anything bad to say about your ex-husband? You're still in love with him?"

I choked on a piece almond and gulped some wine to wash it down. "You really are a detective."

He smiled in response.

"It's complicated," I said. "And you're making it even more so."

"Good. More wine?"

I shook my head. "No, thank you. I'm driving, so I limit myself to one. Besides, I can't stay much longer. I need to get back home."

"Why? Are you worried about something?"

I shook my head but could feel my color rising. I was a terrible liar.

"Why did you ask if Doug Mitchell had ever been arrested? Has he done something that made you think that? Other than lying, that is."

Man, he was good. So again, I tried the truth. "I was just curious. But maybe you should know that he pulled his kids out of school today and shipped them off somewhere."

He frowned. "Really? How do you know this?"

I made a face. "Are you pumping me for information now?"

He shook his head. "No. It's just interesting, that's all."

My wine glass was empty. "My friend, Carol, who works at the library, has a yoga buddy who's the elementary school's secretary. Mt. Abrams is pretty well connected."

"Apparently."

I reached for my purse. "I have to go. I'm sorry. But would you like to do this again?"

"Of course. Next time, a whole dinner?"

I nodded as I got up, and he stood with me. We walked out into the parking lot together, and he waited patiently as I unlocked my car. I felt my heart jump a little.

"Well, thanks."

I could see his smile in the darkness. "You're welcome," he said, and he reached over and drew me towards him. Even with the boots on, I had to stand on my toes, and he bent down to kiss me.

This was not just a pleasant tingle. This was like a jolt of electricity that went right through my boots, into the pavement, and made me grip the fabric of his shirt with both hands. His arms tightened around me, and his strength and heat hit me so hard that when I finally stepped away, I expected to see my clothes fall to the ground in ashes.

"Wow, again," I managed.

"Indeed."

"So, you'll call?" I asked.

"Absolutely."

And I believed him.

There was so much to talk about the next morning that I thought we'd have to walk around the lake twice. Doug had not turned up at the bus stop, and since every mom in Mt. Abrams knew why but didn't want to say anything in front of their children, after the bus left the moms stood in a tight circle, and the speculation ran wild.

I kept my mouth shut. I had a very strong feeling that Doug had run off with his sons because he was frightened of something, and the thought that maybe I was a part of that made me feel queasy. I don't know what he thought I'd done, but somehow, my being in his house set him off.

"Well, you certainly can't blame yourself for anything," Shelly said as we trudged up the hill. Boot was walking as far away from the puddles as she could. What a princess.

"We did break into his house," I said. "I mean, nanny-cam."

"It's interesting though," Carol said. "He could have called the police. If it was about you being in his house, that's what he should have done. But instead, he went after you himself. Very odd behavior."

"Gee, ya think?" Maggie said. "Ellie was scared to death yesterday. That's beyond odd."

"Actually, Doug was scared to death. I wish I hadn't run away from him. Maybe I could have found out what he was so upset about." I tugged Boot's leash.

The rain had kick started spring. It seemed that everything was a few inches taller than it had been just a few days before. The air smelled clean, and the birds were singing, and aside from the nagging at my conscience about Doug, I felt very happy.

And Shelly, who could read me like a book, decided she couldn't hold it in any longer. "And now I want to hear all about your date. Details, woman. Every last one."

I was smiling. I couldn't help it. "I had a lovely time."

Shelly made a noise that suggested complete and utter disgust. "That is not a detail. That's a non-detail."

We reached the top of the hill and rounded the corner when Maggie stopped short.

"He's back," she said, staring at the Mitchell house, sitting on the other side of the lake.

We all looked. The garage door was down. It was only down when Doug was home. Which meant sometime last night, he had returned without his sons.

"I thought he was staying with the sister too," Shelly muttered as we walked quickly towards the clubhouse.

I almost veered off and went home, but that felt cowardly. Doug and I had both behaved badly, and as much as I would have liked to avoid him for the rest of my life, if he were back, avoidance would be highly improbable. Besides, it wasn't like he was sitting on the front porch, watching us.

"Do you think he's watching us?" Shelly wondered aloud. "Like, from the upstairs window there?"

"Thanks, Shel," I said. "He probably had to get clothes and stuff for the boys."

We hurried along the path for a few minutes, then settled back into our usual pace.

"Okay," Carol said. "You were about to give us a blow by blow of your date with Detective Kinali."

"You first," I said. "Didn't you have coffee with Leon?"

She sniffed. "He has allergies. Coffee tomorrow. Your turn."

I took a breath. "He's very interesting. I like talking to him. We laughed, found a few things in common, I think, and we're having dinner together soon. And we shared a most excellent kiss."

"Then why aren't you doing a happy dance?" Shelly asked.

"I'm a little confused," I said "because of Marc."

Maggie frowned. "What about Marc?"

"Well, he told me he still loved me and that he missed me." I took a few steps before I realized everyone else had stopped in their tracks. I turned, and they were all staring at me. "What?"

"Your ex-husband Marc?" Shelly asked. "That miserable piece of—"

"Now, Shelly," Carol broke in. "It's not entirely uncommon for couples to reconnect."

Shelly whirled to face Carol. "After what he put her through?" She then glared at me. "I hope you told him exactly where he could put *that* idea."

"We never got to talk about it. He kissed me then left."

"Kissed you?" Shelly said, her voice rising about an octave.

"Yes. And it was quite a kiss, let me tell you. If it hadn't been so unexpected, we might well have reenacted our entire honeymoon right there on the living room rug."

She marched forward. "Did you tell him about the hottie?"

"Well," I said, getting in step beside her, "I didn't actually use the word hottie, but I did say I had a date."

"And that's when he kissed you?" she asked.

"Yes." I didn't particularly like where the conversation was headed.

"Hmmm," Shelly said.

I glanced back at Maggie. "What do you think?"

"I'm happily married," she said.

"I'm happily married too," Shelly said. "I'm just older and wiser than you, Maggie. Carol was married forever, and I bet even she's rolling her eyes."

"You must admit," Carol said very carefully, "the timing is suspect. On the bright side, you certainly got enough action this week to keep you going for a while."

We walked the rest of the way around the lake in silence. Although I didn't like to think that Marc would really be the kind of man to mess with my head like that, Carol was right. The timing was, at the very least, suspect.

We were nearing the Mitchell house, and my brain suddenly went off in a completely different direction. "He's still there," I said. "Let's hurry."

We picked up the pace as we walked past the house. I had visions of him bursting out of the front door, screaming. Or maybe he was hiding on the porch and would come up behind me.

"Listen," Maggie said.

We stopped. The house was silent. But there was a quiet rumble coming from the garage.

"What is that?" Carol whispered. "A generator?"

Shelly tightened her grip on Buster's leash and as we walked slowly up the drive. "Does that sound like a car engine to you?" she asked.

"Oh, God," Carol breathed. She ran up to the garage, bent, and pulled the door up and open. Maggie was right behind her.

The smell of exhaust almost knocked us over.

Carol turned, her face white. "Call 911. He's in there."

And then Maggie began to scream.

CHAPTER SIX

WE WERE SITTING on the front porch of the Mitchell house. We might have been four women, just sitting and enjoying a beautiful spring morning, but we weren't. We were watching as police cars and emergency vehicles blocked the road. There was yellow tape everywhere. We had been asked by the first officer to arrive to please stay close for questioning.

The whole thing was surreal.

Maggie was still white as a sheet and shaking. Buster growled at every person who walked by. Carol had spent twenty minutes on her cell phone finding someone else to open the library. Shelly left a brief message with her office, then called her husband Mike and started crying on the phone.

I felt numb. I was sitting on the porch step, my arm around Boot's neck, trying not to imagine what was happening in the garage.

A dark unmarked car pulled up, a flashing light in the front window, and a very young-looking man in a dark suit got out of the driver's side.

Sam Kinali got out of the passenger side. He was wearing sunglasses, so I could only watch as his head turned to take in the entire scene. Then, his head stopped turning. He was looking at me.

My arm tightened around Boot, and she whined softly. Carol came down the stairs and walked over to him.

"Oh, thank God, a familiar face," she said. "I'm so glad you're here, Detective Kinali. This is just awful."

He nodded, put his hand on her elbow, and led her back to the porch steps. He took off his glasses and smiled at me. "Are you all right?" he asked.

I nodded several times, but I felt sick to my stomach, guilty and nervous about what he was going to ask, and damn, did he look good in sunglasses.

He reached down, took my hand, and helped me up. Boot growled softly and followed me up the steps and onto the porch.

Carol and I sat down and Sam leaned against the railing. "Ladies, I am Detective Kinali, and this is Detective Monroe. We just need to ask you some questions, and then you'll be free to go."

Detective Monroe took out a pad and pen, looking very serious. Sam smiled.

"Now. Tell me about the morning."

I did not want to be the one to start, so I just huddled further down into the wicker chair, staring at the gray painted floorboards.

Like everything else about the Mitchell house, the porch was picture perfect. A few scattered wicker chairs and Adirondack chairs, painted white, with low scattered tables with potted pansies on them. The perfect place for afternoon lemonade.

"We always walk the same path," Shelly began.

"And you are?" Detective Monroe asked.

Shelly gave her name and phone number, which Detective Monroe copied dutifully. She then turned back to Sam.

"We start at the bottom of the hill after the kids get dropped off from school. We walk across Sommerfield to Morris, take Morris to Davis, and basically crisscross every hill we can until we get up here. We come in from the other side." She pointed to the clubhouse. "Then we walk around the lake and end up back where we started by the clubhouse. Then we all go our own way home."

Sam looked at the clubhouse, then to the other side of the lake. "How long does it take you?"

"It depends," Carol said. "Usually forty-five minutes to an hour. The hills are steep, and we don't rush. Sometimes the dogs slow us down. If it's cold or looks like rain, we go faster."

Sam nodded. "Fine. So today, was anything different?"

We all glanced quickly at each other.

"Well, we knew that Doug had pulled the kids out of school and had told the secretary he was staying at his sisters," Maggie said.

"And how did you know this?" Sam asked, not looking at me.

"Excuse me," Detective Monroe said. "Your name?"

Sam waited patiently, then smiled at Maggie. "Go on."

Maggie looked embarrassed. "Mt. Abrams is a very small community," she said. "Everyone knows pretty much everything that's going on. The secretary at the school is a friend of Carol's, and Carol told me, and well, once I get hold of information…" She blushed. "I have a big mouth."

"Perhaps," Sam said graciously. "Go on."

"Yeah, well, we knew he had taken the boys, so we were kinda surprised that he was home."

"And how did you know he was home?" Sam asked. "Did you knock on the door to speak with him?"

"No," I said. I cleared my throat. "See, the garage doesn't open by itself. You have to get out and pull up the doors. I know, because my garage is the same. When Doug and Lacey went anywhere, they'd leave the doors open so they could just pull in when they returned. So, if the garage doors were closed, they were home."

"And this morning" Sam said, "they were closed."

We nodded.

"So you were walking past, and what, you heard the engine?" His eyes were on me now, and I nodded.

"It gets real quiet up here if there's no one around," I told him. "We weren't talking, so we heard it. At first, Carol thought it was a generator. Then we went up the driveway and realized it was the car, and Carol lifted the door…"

He lifted an eyebrow. "You weren't talking?" he said with a faint smile.

I smiled back. "It can happen."

He nodded. "Did you try to resuscitate the body?"

The body. I swallowed hard.

"No," Carol said. "I looked in the window. He was gone. I could…tell." Her voice cracked just a little.

Sam looked back to the clubhouse, straightened, and turned around. "Stay here," he said as he walked away.

Detective Monroe followed him around the house to the garage.

I took a deep breath. "I have to tell him about Doug and the car and how he grabbed me, and what he said. It might be important."

"You're absolutely right," Maggie said. "Even if we get arrested for breaking into the house."

"We did not," Shelly said, "break in anywhere. The door was wide open. And I agree. Hottie needs to know."

"Can we not," I whispered, "refer to him as *hottie* right now?"

We sat a few minutes more. Buster had fallen asleep, but Boot was restless and kept tugging at the leash and occasionally barking at passersby. And there were a lot of those. In fact, a tiny audience stood front of the Mitchell house, pointing at the four of us and whispering. Kate Fisher was there, and Mary Rose Reed was whispering furiously in her ear, probably giving Kate the entire Mitchell history. Kate kept her eyes on the garage.

"Boy," Maggie muttered, "the jungle drums are going to have a field day with this one."

"I wonder why he did it," Shelly said suddenly. "It doesn't make sense for Doug to kill himself. I always thought he was crazy about those boys. Unless he did kill Lacey and was scared he'd get caught."

"He was scared all right," I said. "But I don't think of getting caught."

Boot growled again, and Sam and Detective Monroe came around the corner and up on the porch. My yellow slicker was in Detective Monroe's hand. Sam looked at me.

"This was found," he said softly, "in the backseat of the car. There's a credit card receipt in the pocket, a few weeks old, for a place called Ezekiel's Tavern. A receipt with your name on it, Ellie. Is there someplace we can go and have a little talk?"

I stood up and nodded. "I live right over there. I'll make us all some coffee." I walked off the porch and past Sam, tugging at Boot's leash.

We sat in the kitchen, of course. Detective Monroe took his coffee black, Sam with milk but no sugar. I sat across from Sam at the table. Carol asked to go down to the library, and Sam gave his permission. Shelly and Maggie were with me, hovering by the refrigerator.

"So, Ellie, what is it you want to tell me?"

Everything. I told him everything, about going into the house and finding her clothes gone, about the video camera, about Doug giving me a lift the morning before. Sam sat quietly, his hands folded, listening intently. Detective Monroe took notes. Sam just watched me with fierce concentration.

When I finally stopped talking, I took a long, uneven breath. "I would have told you this all last night," I said, "but I didn't want to get anyone in trouble. And I didn't think Doug would kill himself."

Detective Monroe looked up from his notebook. "What? What happened last night?"

Sam didn't take his eyes off my face. "Ms. Rocca and I had a drink last night. Purely social, John. Nothing at all to do with this case." He finally looked away and turned to John. "Have them look for that video camera. And check to see if any other cameras were hidden in the house. As soon as the sister has been notified, let me know. We need to speak to her ASAP. Have Mike treat this as a suspicious death. Don't just assume suicide."

Detective Monroe stood, fished his cell phone out of his pocket, and walked out onto the back porch.

I leaned forward across the table. "Suspicious death?"

Sam met my eye. He paused for a minute, thinking, then spoke. "Douglas Mitchell was a man afraid of something. So much so that he moved his children to what I imagine he felt was a safer place. And then he killed himself? Does that make sense to you?"

I shook my head. "No, I guess not. But what if he thought he was going to get caught for killing Lacey?"

He shook his head. "You're back to that? Why would he kill her?"

"For five million dollars?" I said.

Shelly spoke up. "It's the only motive for him killing himself that makes sense. If she just left with the money, why would he do it?"

He nodded. "That's true. I made a call after you came to see me, Ellie. Lacey and Doug both inherited. The boys received a million each in trust. The rest was evenly divided between husband and wife." He shrugged. "It was still a sizable amount for both of them. And here's the thing. Their joint account was emptied yesterday. All the money, and there was quite a bit, believe me, was transferred to an off-shore account."

We sat, letting that sink in.

"So, one of them wanted it all," I said.

Sam nodded. "Apparently."

"It couldn't have been Doug," I said.

"Why not?" Sam asked.

"Because the only explanation for Doug saying what he said yesterday is that he gave Lacey his share of the money, but she wanted something more," I said.

Sam nodded. "True."

"How did Lacey's father die?" Shelly asked.

Sam glanced at her. "He was a diabetic. The apparent cause of death was an insulin overdose. By the time 911 was called and he was taken to the hospital, nothing could be done."

Maggie and Shelly both came forward, grabbed chairs, and sat.

"Very Sunny Von Bulow," Shelly said.

Sam, clearly amused, nodded. "Yes."

"Was he alone? When he overdosed, I mean?" Maggie asked.

"No," Sam answered. "His wife, Millicent, was with him."

"Wait," I said excitedly. "I thought we decided she was no longer in the picture."

He threw back his head and laughed. "We? Who's this we?"

Detective Monroe returned. "Detective Kinali?"

Sam pushed away from the table and stood. "Ladies, thank you for all your assistance. We'll put a call out for Lacey's car. She is a person of interest. If nothing else, we need to inform her of her husband's death. We'll find her. We usually do." He smiled down at me and left.

Shelly exhaled loudly. "Lacey is the bad guy. Who knew? I feel so bad now, for thinking all those terrible things about

Doug." She shook her head sadly. "Those poor little boys."

"I know," I said. "That's really creepy to think that Lacey came back here and did this."

Maggie shuddered. "Don't say that. I won't be able to sleep as it is. But I gotta say, that is one sexy man."

I grinned. "I know. He's nice too, and interesting to talk to." Something hit me, and I stopped grinning. "Did Millicent kill him?"

"Who? Lacey's father?" Shelly waved a hand. "Why would she? *She* wasn't getting any money."

"Maybe she didn't know that," I said. "Maybe she *thought* she was getting all the money."

"Did she kill Lacey?" Maggie asked.

Shelly looked disgusted. "If Lacey had been killed, don't you think Doug would have gone to the police? Instead of lying to us? No, I think Lacey lit out of here on her own, then came back and killed Doug."

"But why?" I asked. "She already got everything."

We sat there in silence until we heard the sound of a siren. We got up and went to the front door in time to see an ambulance pull out of the Mitchells' driveway.

Good-bye, Doug.

CHAPTER SEVEN

WHEN MT. ABRAMS was still a baby, rather than a full-grown community, a small town center had gone up, consisting of a post office, a firehouse, and a large public park called, in a complete stroke of originality, Main Park. It was right below Elliot Street, where Josiah had built the second wave of homes. I lived on Abrams Lane at the very top of the hill, and farther from the lake than the Mitchells lived. While the clubhouse was the social hub of the community during the summer, this little bit of quaintness was the year-round center for gathering information, real or imagined.

Over the years, they built a library in Main Park, right where Sommerfield Drive split Main Park in two. The post office was modernized, but the firehouse was deemed too small and inadequate. So a modern firehouse was built along State Road 51, and the original firehouse became the community hall. The Mount Abrams Homeowners Association met there, as well as the Garden Club, Historical Society, a few Girl Scout troops, one church group, Weight Watchers, and a local crafting club. Two book clubs also met there, so as not to crowd out the library. For a 120-year-old building with undependable heat, no air conditioner, and antiquated toilets, it was a pretty happening spot.

I could actually see the roof of the old firehouse from my back kitchen window and probably looked at it a dozen times every day, but I had forgotten all about the Garden Club until I got a text from Lynn Fahey around five o'clock.

C U at Garden Club 7:30

I texted back.

Maybe not. Doug Mitchell killed self. I found him.

Lynn was quick to respond.

OMG! Terrible. R u guarding the body or something?

I stared at her text.

NO. Happened this am.

Then you can still come

Ah Lynn, the soul of compassion and empathy. I texted her back that I'd be there, then texted Shelly and Maggie, and guilted them into meeting me. Cait was working, so Tessa grudgingly agreed to come with me, promising to sit quietly in a corner and read.

The meeting was not what I needed. I felt physically exhausted and emotionally drained. Doug had killed himself. Or Lacey killed him. Either way, I felt right in the middle of it all, and it was not a pleasant place to be.

Shelly and her husband Mike were already seated when Tessa and I got there. The place was packed. I handed over my fivedollar membership fee and got my official Garden Club card. I spotted Maggie and Viv in the back row. I pushed Tessa towards the small alcove where she could sit and read her book, and then started back towards Maggie, but Kate Fisher suddenly popped up.

"I saw you this morning," she said breathlessly. "You all found him?"

I did not want to talk about Doug and this morning, least of all to Kate. I looked at her.

She was at least sixty, I guessed, with pale hair fading to gray. She was fairly tall and slender, attractive, with blue eyes and an open, easy smile. I could have liked her, if only she'd have kept her mouth shut every once in a while.

"I was there, of course," she went on. "Watching with everyone else. How horrible. They're all saying that you heard the car engine running? It's almost like God sent you to find him. I didn't know them at all, of course, but how tragic. Two little boys, right? And Mrs. Mitchell? Just gone? You talked to the police afterward, didn't you? Did they say anything about finding the poor wife?"

She paused for breath, so I jumped in. "No, Kate, the police didn't say anything about Lacey." Not that I would have told *her* anything if they had.

"That beautiful house, that beautiful family, destroyed by one selfish act. Oh, my heart bleeds, it really does. And to think it happened right here, in quiet Mt. Abrams. You know, when I found this house up here, Paul, you know Paul Malone, my landlord? Well Paul told me that this was the perfect place to live, safe and peaceful. Who knew that something like this could happen? I guess it was lucky the little boys weren't there. Could you imagine? What will become of them now?

All that money can't bring their parents back. Poor little lambs."

She had wound down again, so I nodded, murmured something appropriate, and backed away. I hurried to sit with Maggie and Viv.

Maggie was grinning. "Get an earful?"

"Lord, that woman can run her mouth," I whispered. I looked around. "Who are all these people? I don't recognize half of them."

Viv started pointing fingers and naming names. At least a dozen new faces had moved into Mt. Abrams in the past two years, and Viv had handled their transactions. They were mostly younger couples with no children, drawn to Mt. Abrams by its proximity to the train and lower tax rates.

"How did Lynn track them all down?" I asked.

Maggie made a face. "Maybe these are Mary Rose's people."

"No, this is all Lynn's doing," Viv said. "That woman could lead a priest into a whorehouse."

I stared at Viv. "Is that a real saying?"

She made a face. "It is for me."

The meeting started out in a rather orderly fashion, welcoming all the new members (we had to stand up and introduce ourselves) going over the minutes, and handing out the agenda. The library paver question was the fifth item down under Old Business.

"You mean we gotta sit through all this?" Viv groused. "I wanted to just vote and go."

Maggie shushed her. She had lived in Brooklyn her whole life, and found small-town machinations fascinating.

"I mean seriously, what four other things could these people be talking about?" Viv continued. "Mt. Abrams isn't that big."

"Viv," I said, "did you happen to notice when that power of attorney was dated?"

She frowned for a moment. "You're talking about Doug Mitchell? I think it was just the day or two before."

"And it had to be notarized, right?"

She nodded.

There was something stuck in my brain, something that wasn't making sense. "When did he call about putting the house on the market?"

"That Friday. Right after lunch. Why?"

Maggie turned away from Mary Rose, who was standing at the podium arguing about peat moss, and nudged me with her foot.

"What are you thinking?" she asked.

"Okay," I said slowly, thinking aloud. "That power of attorney, he could not have gotten it without her signing as well, right?"

Viv nodded. "That's right. It has to be signed by both parties in the presence of the notary."

"So they were in it together. They had to be. So something must have happened, and they *both* decided to sell the house." I suddenly realized something. "And the bank account. Sam said it had been emptied. They both needed to do that, too." I looked at Maggie. "Do you remember if she seemed different Friday when she got the boys? Think, Maggie. Like she knew she was going to have to leave them?"

Maggie frowned. "I don't know, Ellie. She never seemed excited or upset or very emotional about anything. But nothing struck me funny about Friday afternoon."

The gavel banged, and we all looked to the front of the hall. Mary Rose had raised her voice. Next item—the pavers for the library park.

Mary Rose was a throwback. Her hair was bluish silver and permed, and she dressed in a pantsuit with matching accessories to walk around the block. She had been running the Garden Club for years and grew peonies in her tiny back yard. Until Lynn Fahey had started disagreeing with her, she had pretty much been responsible for every tree, bush, and flower planted in Mt. Abrams. Seven years ago, Lynn suggested that the Garden Club had no right to tell people what they could and could not grow in their own yards, and if Beverly Sutter wanted to plant bamboo, she should plant bamboo, even if it wasn't in keeping with the general look of the community. Lynn and Mary Rose had been at war ever since.

Mary Rose presented a very compelling case. According to her, even a rise in humidity caused the area around the picnic table to become a muddy disaster. Not only would pavers keep the area cleaner, it would visually broaden the walkway and mean less maintenance for Craig, our grounds manager, in that he would not have to move the tables when he mowed the grass. Mary Rose was an excellent speaker, and I found myself nodding in agreement with everything she said.

Then Lynn got up, pointing out that the walkway was already five feet wide, how could there be grass under the picnic tables if Mary Rose kept insisting the area was a dust bowl, and that Craig was *paid* to move the picnic tables when he mowed, so what was the big frigging deal? She then launched into her Death By Rock Salt argument.

Mary Rose did not take it well. New members asked to be recognized, and the discussion seemed pretty fairly divided.

My mind was on other things. "Viv, who notarized Doug's POA? Do you remember?"

Viv nodded. "Sure. It was Mary Rose. She's the only notary in town. You gonna talk to her?"

I nodded. "Yes. Maybe they said something to her. I don't know."

Maggie frowned. "Why is this bothering you so much?" she asked.

"Because I feel like if I had talked to Doug, tried to make sense of what he was saying, I could have helped in some way," I said.

Viv shook her head. "Don't even start thinkin' like that. If Doug chose to kill himself, it had nothing to do with you. If Lacey killed him, it also had nothing to do with you. If anything, Doug took those boys and put them in a safe place because of you. Think about that."

Voices were starting to get louder, so I tried to pay attention. As with all small groups run by people with either big egos or plagued by self-esteem issues, *Roberts Rules of Order* were quickly replaced with name calling and general mayhem. Emma McLaren, self-appointed witch of Mt. Abrams, started telling everyone that the very earth beneath the library had a life of its own and needed to breathe. That was apparently the last straw, because someone finally stood up, and yelling over the raised voices, made a motion that pavers be put down in the library park. I jumped up and seconded the motion.

Mary Rose and Lynn were clearly not through tearing each other's eyes out, but there was a motion on the floor, and they had to shut up. By a show of hands, the motion was clearly defeated. The hydrangeas were safe for another year.

We did not stay for the aftermath. I stood up, motioned to Tessa, and we scurried out of there, followed by Maggie and Viv.

We stood on the street, Tessa and I headed in one direction, Viv and Maggie going down the hill.

"Are you going to talk to Mary Rose?" Maggie asked.

I nodded. "Tomorrow. Come with?"

"You bet," Maggie said, and started walking.

"Can I come too?" Viv called.

"Sure," I answered back.

"That was boring," Tessa said. "This is a boring place to live."

I grabbed her little hand and squeezed it. "Not anymore, baby. Not anymore."

Mary Rose lived in one of the ranch houses that had been built in the fifties, down the hill and closer to Route 51. It was below Sommerfield Drive which was the dividing line between old and new Mt. Abrams. Among the old guard of Mt. Abrams, living in the new section meant you lacked a certain status, but it also meant you had a real yard, a garage, and an electrical system that could be counted on in all weather conditions.

Mary Rose's yard looked like a cover for *Better Homes and Gardens*. There were daffodils and all sorts of bulbs popping up everywhere, bushes were budding, the Japanese maple was leafing out, and there were no stray leaves or bits of branch to spoil the green sweep of her lawn.

"How does she keep this so clean?" Maggie muttered.

"I don't think she has much else to do," I answered.

Mary Rose opened the door at our knock but did not look particularly pleased to see us. I didn't think she would have been able to see us last night, all the way in the back row, but she did not greet us as fellow paver-lovers.

"Yes? Can I help you with something?" She was dressed in a skirt, blouse, hose, and heels. Her clip-on earrings matched her pin. At nine in the morning. Maggie and I had come straight from our walk, dropped off Boot and picked up Viv, and were still slightly sweaty and disheveled.

"Hi, Mary Rose," I said, smiling. "I know this is going to sound odd, but can I talk to you about Lacey and Doug Mitchell?"

Immediately, her entire demeanor changed. She opened the door, her eyes bright. "Come in, please. I have coffee on."

Her house was immaculate, frozen in the eighties, and there were plastic runners covering the beige wall-to-wall carpet. We followed her into her kitchen, and sat at her round maple table, in matching captain's chairs.

"I must say," she said as she took coffee cups and saucers from the cabinet, "I was quite surprised to see you at the Garden Club meeting last night, Ellie." Having walked past my yard, she was perfectly justified in saying that.

"Yes. Well, Cait may be going to France, and since she's the one who usually looks after the garden, I thought I should maybe get some help." I stumbled over the lie, of course, but Mary Rose didn't seem to notice.

"You have a garden?" she asked. I was so used to drinking coffee from either a mug or a Starbucks take-away cup that the shallow cup and matching saucer looked antique.

"Sort of. Like I said, I'm going to try to work a little harder at it."

"And you, Maggie?" Mary Rose poured coffee from a Corning Ware coffee pot, pristine white and embellished with a single blue flower. I had never seen one in real life, except at garage sales and thrift stores.

Another legitimate question. Maggie lived in one of the converted summer cottages, long and narrow with roughly twelve inches of yard between her front porch and the curb. Those twelve inches were planted with hostas. The space between her house and the houses on the other side was so narrow that simple pavers had been laid down, creating a dark path barely wide enough to get through. Her back yard consisted of a small deck and two parking spaces.

But Maggie had no qualms about her motives. "I just came to support Lynn. I'm a hydrangea lover."

Viv smiled. "Me too."

Mary Rose sniffed and put the coffee pot back on the stove, giving us her back a little longer than was probably necessary.

She sat with us. "Yes. Well, what were you saying? About the Mitchells? I saw you there yesterday morning, Ellie. You too, Maggie. It must have been awful."

I nodded. "Yes. But I want to ask you about the power of attorney you notarized for them last week."

She took a long sip of coffee and looked thoughtful. "They came to my door just as Fred was coming back, so that was about ten o'clock." Fred was her husband, who every morning, no matter what the weather, walked from Mt. Abrams to the CVS way down on Route 51. It was said you could set your clock by his coming and going, so if Mary Rose said ten o'clock, you could bet she was dead on.

"They were very nervous. Apparently, she had printed off the form on the computer, and they were very anxious to have it notarized," Mary Rose said.

"Excited nervous or scared nervous?" I asked.

Mary Rose narrowed her eyes and thought hard. "Scared. He was scared. In fact, at one point, she put her arms around him, to comfort him. She kept telling him it would be fine."

"What would be fine?" Maggie asked.

Mary Rose lifted her shoulders, then let them drop. "I have no idea. They were very secretive people, you know. I don't think anyone really knew them. I'd invited them to join Garden Club, of course, but Lacey said they weren't joiners." She raised her eyebrows. "Did you know anything about them?"

Viv shook her head. "I sold them the house three years ago, and signed the contract to sell it again, and I don't even think I exchanged ten words with them in between."

"They were not," Mary Rose said, "very good neighbors."

"Was she scared as well?" I asked.

Mary Rose shook her head. "Not so much. In fact, she was in control of the situation. She had the paperwork, had filled in most of it before they got here, and told him where to sign. She seemed in a hurry."

Maggie looked at me. "They sign the power of attorney, call Viv, then what? Why was she in a hurry?"

I had been watching Mary Rose, and she leaned forward. "What do you ladies know that the rest of us don't?"

"Nothing," I said. I stood up. "Thank you, Mary Rose. For the coffee and information."

She got up in a hurry. "Ellie, wait now. What's going on?"

"Nothing, Mary Rose. Honestly. We were just curious about what happened that might have caused Lacey to leave so suddenly."

Mary Rose folded her arms across her chest. "Leave? Who said she left? I'm betting Lacey disappeared because her husband killed her, and then killed himself out of guilt."

I made my way to the front door. "You're probably right. Thank you, Mary Rose."

We hurried down her walk and up the street.

"So, what are we thinking?" Maggie asked.

"I'm thinking that we need to know what happened after the boys got picked up by the bus. Between then and ten, they saw something or heard something that shook them up," I said.

"Or not," Viv said. "Maybe he made it all up. Maybe he did it just to get her to sign, so he could kill her."

"Or maybe *she* made it up so she had an excuse to get the hell outta Dodge," Maggie said.

"But when he was talking to me, he said something like he didn't know she had made friends. That she was using me. If he wasn't talking about Lacey, who else could it have been?" I asked. The more I thought about what had happened, the more confused I got.

"Well, since it's easier to find out if something did happen than if something didn't, where should we start looking?" Maggie asked.

"Oh girl," Viv said. "You have to ask? The post office."

"I have to see my mother this morning," I said. "Do you think—"

Viv grinned. "Leave this to us, Ellie. We've got this covered."

CHAPTER EIGHT

MY MOTHER'S ASSISTED living facility nestled at the foot of a gently rolling hillside in Sussex County. It was an old mansion that had been carefully converted, added on to, improved, and improved again until it met all the state safety standards, yet still managed to look like a very rich person's gracious country estate. Mom had a room on the second floor. Large and sunny, she had a narrow bed, all her books and pictures, her phone chair and a small television. In the bay window was her dresser and another chair, and that's where I sat, every Friday before going down to have lunch.

We had once been able to go out for lunch, but last year she went to the ladies room at a local Panera, wandered past where we were sitting, out the door, and was found three hours later, sitting in the middle of the freezer aisle of a Pathmark almost a mile away.

Now, we had lunch in the common dining room, which was not a bad thing. Aside from the excellent food, the other residents were more or less delightful characters who put on a never-ending floorshow for their guests.

We sat at a table next to the nimble-fingered Justine Caldwell, who barely had the strength to hold her fork. My mother kept glaring at the poor woman, who, since she was fairly deaf, just smiled and nodded. After lunch we walked around the grounds for about half an hour before going back inside and upstairs. My mother became agitated, as she often did when she sensed my visit coming to a close.

"Justine is taking all my Agatha Christies," she muttered.

"Mom, how is she even getting up the stairs?" I asked.

My mother sat in her phone chair, rocking back and forth. She was still a lovely woman, her thick hair almost completely gray, her big, dark eyes angry and confused. I had inherited her creamy skin and thick, perfectly shaped eyebrows, for which I will be eternally grateful, as well as her stubby fingers and love of eating, for which I was not so grateful. Now, I could feel her irritation growing. Sometimes I just kissed her good-bye and she'd smile happily. Lately though, our partings were getting harder.

"And I don't know why I can't just live with you. I know Marc wouldn't mind."

"Mom, you need to be with somebody all the time now. You know that. I can't watch you. I have to work."

"You work from home," she whined.

"Yes, until I'm off at a conference or a festival or meeting with a client somewhere," I said. My arguments didn't matter to her. She'd heard them all before. She just didn't remember them.

"This is a terrible place. They do bad things here."

"No, Mom, they don't. You love it here."

"And the food is awful. Gruel."

I sighed and picked up my purse. One of the aides, Liz, poked her head in. "Leona," she called loudly, "we're getting ready for cards downstairs. You want to come with me?"

My mother's head snapped around. "Yes. Yes, I love cards." She waved in my direction as she got up. "See you tomorrow, Ellie. Give your babies a kiss for me."

I smiled gratefully at Liz, who took my mother's arm and led her out of the room.

I sat there for a few minutes more. My high school graduation picture was on one of her shelves. I looked at it closely. I was a very pretty girl back then, pretty enough to have had lots of young men offer me beer and pot and sex. In the spirit of the seventies, which was when I had come of age, I took many of them up on their offers.

That was then. This was now. I closed the door behind me when I left my mother's room.

Sam Kinali called while I was walking down to get Tessa at the bus stop.

"How are you?" he asked, like he actually meant it.

"I'm fine. What have you found out?"

"I'm fine too, thanks for asking," he said, laughter in his voice. "I realize it's short notice, but can I take you out for dinner this evening?"

"Cait is working, and on a Friday night on such short notice, getting a sitter for Tessa might be tough." I tried to remember what was in my freezer besides Smart

Ones frozen meals, sugar-free ice pops and Cait's chicken potpies. "How do you feel about spaghetti and meatballs?"

"Two of my favorite things."

"I have homemade sauce, and I'll get some salad. About seven?"

"I'll bring wine and dessert," he said, and hung up.

Damn. Dessert.

Tessa and I made a quick run through Stop and Shop, and only spent one hundred and forty seven dollars. That little girl grabbed everything her little arms could reach. When we got home, I pulled the sauce and meatballs out of the freezer, put away everything but the salad fixings and the box of pasta, and quickly dusted the dining room. The girls and I ate in the kitchen, and the weekly housekeeping routine tended to be a little lax.

Cait came down, dressed for work, halfway through the process. "You're dusting? Are we expecting the queen?"

"No. Sam Kinali."

"Do you like him?"

"Do you like Kyle Lieberman?"

"Fair enough," she said, and left without further comment.

The sauce was still frozen when I threw it in the pot, but by ten to seven, it was bubbling gently, and the house smelled amazing. It had been my mother's recipe, and every time I made it I remembered Sunday dinners when my father was alive, and he and my mother were still in love after thirty years.

"Why are we having the policeman over to dinner?" Tessa finally got around to asking. "And why did you change? Is this a date?"

"No," I lied. I did not want Tessa to start getting attached to anyone, or think that I was. "But after we eat, you are going to excuse yourself from the table and go upstairs and watch TV up in the spare room. We may be discussing grown-up things."

"Like that dead Mr. Mitchell?"

I nodded. "Maybe."

"Is there a mad killer on the loose in Mt. Abrams?"

I shook my head. "No, there is not. And if there was, we have the worlds most protective dog to scare anyone away, right?"

She nodded. "Can I bring popcorn?"

"Yes."

"And Oreos?"

"No. Just popcorn. And if you don't behave, I'll return the Oreos and all the other junk you bought today. Understand?"

She nodded.

The doorbell rang exactly at seven. I hurried to answer, opening the door to find Maggie and Viv standing there, looking excited and each holding a bottle of wine.

"What are you doing here?" I asked, trying not to look disappointed.

"Don't you want to hear what we found out today about Lacey Mitchell?" Maggie asked.

Before I could answer, I saw Sam Kinali step up on the porch behind them. He had a bottle of wine in one hand, and what looked to be a bakery box in the other. "I'd love to," he said.

Viv turned around and immediately got it. "Come on, Maggie, we'll come back another time."

Maggie, however, missed all the clues. "Detective Kinali, what luck. We found some very interesting things out today. They might help your case."

My shoulders slumped as Viv poked Maggie with her elbow. "No, Maggie. Let's take our wine to Shelly's house. We'll talk to Ellie later."

"Please, ladies. Don't let me run you off," Sam said, his eyes dancing. "I find all this amateur sleuthing very entertaining. Unless, Ellie, dinner is ready right this minute?"

He was something else. "No. I haven't even put the pasta on," I said. "But it's a beautiful night, let's stay out here on the porch. I'll get glasses and a corkscrew."

"Here," Sam said, openly grinning now. I recognized the box. Pirelli's Bakery. I knew Pirelli's. They made things filled with sugar and cream and candied fruits.

I was doomed.

They were all laughing quite companionably when I went back out on the porch, holding a tray of glasses and a bowl of pita chips. Sam was enjoying himself very much. Viv rolled her eyes apologetically and grabbed the corkscrew, opening her bottle of wine. She poured, and we all drank. I introduced Sam and Viv, but they already seemed like fast friends.

The evening was starting to cool off, but the air smelled fresh and clean, with the faint scent of lilacs, and it was still light. I looked out towards the lake, and of course, the Mitchell house. There was still yellow crime scene tape everywhere.

Sam snagged a pita chip and motioned towards Maggie. "So tell us, what did you find out?"

Maggie cleared her throat. "Well, we talked to Joanie. Joan Dudley, down at the post office. That's kind of the information hub out here, if you know what I mean."

Joan was something over seventy, and had been postmistress for fifty years. She heard every single word that was spoken in the post office, even if it wasn't spoken to her. We often joked that if she could, she'd have tables and chairs in the lobby so that people could sit down and gossip longer. As it was, she pretty much knew everything that was going on in town.

"Lacey came in every morning at the same time," Maggie went on. "I guess right after she came up from the bus stop. Joanie said that she was always polite, never chatted, and didn't get a lot of junk mail. She also said that Doug brought the boys in every Saturday, and that he was much friendlier, but still not much for idle chitchat." She leaned confidentially towards Sam. "Joanie lives for idle chitchat."

Sam nodded encouragingly. "I see."

"Anyway, Joanie noticed that Lacey had a postcard from the library, the ones they send to tell you a book you've reserved has come in, so she thought that's where Lacey went next. So we went there as well."

Sam drank some wine. "And?"

Viv took over. "Carol said that yes, Lacey was there Friday morning. And she did pick up a book. But then something weird happened. Kate Fisher and Lynn Fahey were talking about something, probably the damn Garden Club, and Carol said that Lacey just kind of froze and listened. Kate has a big mouth, just so you know. Not only does she talk a lot, but she's loud. Whatever Lacey heard, Carol said she turned white and practically ran out of the library."

Sam's eyes narrowed. "Really? And Carol—this is Carol Anderson, yes?— didn't remember what the conversation was about?"

Maggie and Viv both shook their heads.

"We were going to Carol's tonight and ask her," Viv said, "but she's got a hot date as well."

Sam grinned, and I gulped my entire glass of wine.

Viv stood up. "Well, hate to leave, but we'll take our bottle here and go tell Shelly what we've learned. Maybe we can all talk to Carol tomorrow, Ellie?"

I stood up, and so did Sam.

"Great idea," I said.

"It was a real pleasure talking to you ladies," Sam said, bowing graciously. Maggie giggled as she and Viv walked off into the evening.

Sam and I settled back down. My solar lights went on. My front porch wasn't as neat and chic as the Mitchells porch. My furniture was older and a bit creaky, but I had painted it all last year, and the cushions had been dusted off. If was cozy and comfortable, and with the view of the lake, it was one of my favorite places on earth.

"This must be a good life for you." Sam said softly. "I can smell your spaghetti sauce from here. Good food, a beautiful lake, and friends who come by with wine."

"Yes," I said. "I'm very lucky. This is a good place to live. I'll put on the pasta. I'll be right back."

Inside the house, I turned up the water for the pasta, lit a few candles, and turned on some music. Tessa made a face at me from her reading chair in the living room, and I stuck my tongue out at her as I went by.

Boot followed me back on the porch. She growled softly at Sam, who patted her on the head and behind her ears, making them friends for life. She hopped up on a chair and sat back, ready to join the conversation.

"I suppose it's terribly unprofessional to talk about an active case?" I asked.

Sam nodded. "It is indeed. But Lawrence isn't too strict about things. The preliminary autopsy shows that Doug Mitchell may have been injected with something prior to his death by asphyxiation. There were no signs of struggle or any other trauma, which indicates he sat there quietly in the car until he passed out. We have to wait for toxicology reports before we can determine what, if anything, was in his system. That will determine whether he either did, in fact, kill himself, or if he was drugged and murdered."

"When will you know for sure?"

"Hopefully by tomorrow. In the mean time, we're looking for Lacey."

"She's a suspect?"

He shifted in his seat. "When a person is murdered, the spouse always gets looked at very closely."

I nodded. A few cars had gone by, and the clubhouse on the lake suddenly lit up.

"What's going on there?" Sam asked.

"That's the lake clubhouse. Every Mother's Day, the Historical Society holds a brunch, a fundraiser for Founder's Day Weekend. They're over there now, starting to get ready."

"That sounds nice."

"It is. I take my mom every year. The food is good; it's lots of fun for my girls, and you can't beat eating out by the lake on a beautiful spring morning." I stood up. "Ready for dinner?"

We went inside. Tessa was solemn and polite. The dinner was delicious. Sam and I finished the second bottle of wine, and inside the bakery box were perfect little butter cookies that melted in your mouth, and after months of sugar depravation, may have been the best tasting cookies ever. I made espresso, and Sam and I sat at the dining room table, talking and laughing, and when he left, he gave me a goodnight kiss that did more than send electricity to my toes—it sent all sorts of other feelings to all sorts of other parts of my body. This was a man who really knew his way around a woman, and I was pretty sure I wanted him to get to know mine a lot better, and the sooner the better.

It wasn't until I was going to bed that I saw the text from Marc. Asking about Sunday, with a little heart emoji at the end.

CHAPTER NINE

SHELLY CALLED ME first thing Saturday morning.

"How was your dinner? Viv and Maggie came over from your place last night, and we drank ourselves silly."

"My date was terrific. Really. He is a lovely man, and we talked forever, and I had pasta and butter cookies. Pretty much the perfect night."

"Great," she said. "When are we going to talk to Carol?"

The library closed at one on Saturdays, so Shelly and I met up with Carol as she was locking up. She saw us and rolled her eyes.

"Are you here to torment me about the Friday Lacey Mitchell was in the library?"

We fell into step beside her. "Yes," I said. "But first tell us about Leon."

Her eyes lit up. "He's nice," she said. "Almost seventy, widowed for twelve years, golfs three times a week, and thinks John Updike is overrated. We had quite a bit in common and agreed to have a longer date next week. Possibly even dinner." She glanced sideways at me. "And I hear you had some company?"

I nodded. "Yes. Sam Kinali and I are getting along very well, thank you very much, although we did not discuss Updike."

Carol sighed. "Do find out what he reads, Ellie. How else will you know what kind of person he really is?"

"She will," Shelly broke in. "Now what about Lacey?"

Carol lived on Sommerfield in a 1920s Craftsman with lots of beams and a deep porch. We climbed the steps and sat down on weathered teak chairs.

"Can I get you anything?" she asked, and when we nodded, she closed her eyes and took a couple of deep breaths. "She had reserved the Cleopatra biography that came out a number of years ago. I had it brought in from another branch. She checked out the book, and we were standing at the desk, talking about it, when suddenly Kate Fisher laughed very loudly about something; you know how she can be." Carol frowned. "I think Kate and Lynn had been over by the computers in the back, and they were walking towards the front. Lynn was not, I don't think, talking about those stupid pavers. It was something about Mother's Day. The brunch."

She sat up, and her face changed. "Yes. She wanted Kate to help with the brunch, and Kate said something about her own daughter living in California. She had a question about when the boathouse was going to open, and Lynn said next week. Kate started saying she always wanted to learn to sail, and then she was off about boats; you know how she always talks like she knows everything. And in seconds, Lacey turned white and broke into a cold sweat and practically ran out." Carol sighed happily. "That was it. The brunch and the boathouse."

Shelly and I looked at each other.

"What on earth," Shelly said slowly, "could have scared Lacey about the boathouse opening up?"

"Or Mother's Day?" I said. "Lacey was at the last Mother's Day brunch. She sat at our table. My mother thought her little boys were adorable."

Carol shrugged. "I have no idea. Then Kate and Lynn checked out their books, and Lynn made a comment about Lacey rushing off, and Kate asked about her, Lacey I mean, and if I knew her at all, and I told her that none of us knew her very well." Carol shook her head. "I wonder where she is. If she ran away from Doug for some reason, surely she would have come back by now for her sons, no?"

"This hasn't been very helpful," I said. "But thanks anyway, Carol. And good for you and Leon."

She smiled happily. "Yes. Leon. There may be something there. Are you sure I can't get you ladies anything? I can make coffee."

Shelly and I both shook our heads and left. We walked in silence until we turned up towards Davis Road.

"I wonder if Kate's home?" I said, half to myself.

"She's always home," Shelly said. "She has no visible means of support that I know of. All she does is roam around in search someone to talk to."

"Still. I think I'll wander over. Talk to you later." Shelly continued up the hill, and I walked towards Kate's house.

There was something bothering me, but it was so far in the back of my mind I couldn't quite reach it. I stepped onto her tiny porch and knocked.

She opened the door and smiled. "Hello, Ellie. What a surprise! She pushed open the screen door and stepped outside. "Where are your friends? I swear you girls are just like a pack of kittens, running all over town together. All alone? My, is everything all right?"

"I just wanted to ask you, Kate, did you know Lacey Mitchell before you moved here?"

That stopped her. Her mouth dropped open and nothing came out. Then she shook herself. "What a question! Why don't you come on in. I'll make us some tea."

Her house was like a staged photo shoot. Lots of chintz and soft pastels, ferns, and small white candles everywhere. No family pictures. No shoes kicked to a corner or magazines spread open on a side table.

It looked just like the Mitchell house had looked.

Then I remembered something she'd said.

"Kate, how did you know about the money?"

She scooted right by me, off to the back of the house.

"I have this wonderful green leaf tea, so flavorful. I get it from a little specialty shop in Boston. Pricey, yes, but so worth it. I do love a good cup of tea, don't you?"

I followed her into the kitchen. Again, clean and perfect. Even the towels, hanging on hooks, were spotless.

"At the Garden Club meeting, Kate, remember? You said something about all that money not being able to bring the parents back. How did you know about the money?"

"Because it should have been mine, dear. All mine. I was married to that man for years. I really did deserve *something* from that miserable son of a bitch. Why do you think I killed him in the first place?"

I took two steps back and felt my heart in my throat. Her blue eyes were perfectly calm, her smile sincere. But the air in the room had changed, and I was suddenly very afraid.

She took a long breath. "That was probably more information than you wanted to hear," she said. "Honestly, Ellie, I have to tell you the strain of the past few weeks has really taken a toll on my nerves. Now, about that tea. Honey or sugar?"

There were two ways out of her kitchen, back the way we came, through the living room, or through the screened back door. The back door was closer, but I'd have to get past her. Running through the whole house would put her behind me, and I wasn't sure that was a good idea.

I cleared my throat. "Honey. Please."

She beamed. "I love honey too. Put it on everything, even my toast in the morning." She turned away from me again, pulling two pink mugs from the cabinet and adjusting the kettle on the stove. I moved slowly towards the right. The back door was barely ten feet away. God bless old houses and their tiny rooms, I thought. I could easily make it to the door…

I took another step towards the door, and she hit me. It happened so fast I barely registered her lifting her arm as her hand became a fist. I tried to turn away, and I almost made it, but she hit me. Her knuckles went into my cheek, and the pain was incredible. I staggered back, holding my hand to my face. I could feel blood running from my nose, and my eye began to swell.

She shook her hand. Her knuckles were red. "Oh dear, I'm going to have to put some ice on my hand. Will you look at that? I'll be sore for days."

I was trying not to faint. I took a deep breath, counted to three, then exhaled slowly. Again. And again. She had hit me

"Are you crazy?" I blurted. "What did you do that for?"

Her eyes narrowed, and she rushed towards me, her face inches from mine. "Don't call me that," she said, very quietly. "I'm not crazy."

"Then what do you call it?" I hollered, stepping back from her as far as I could. "Why else would you hit me?"

I watched as she carefully rearranged her face, stepped back from me and smoothed down the front of her dress with her hands.

"I'm sorry, Ellie. That was very…wrong of me. But I can't let you leave." She smiled at me, a brittle, frightening smile. No, she wasn't going to let me leave. Ever.

I tried to think. I needed to put her at ease, get her to let her guard down. Right now I could see that she was still so tightly wound that one wrong move, and she'd probably be all over me again.

I pitched my voice down and tried to sound not completely terrified. "Why not, Kate?"

"Well, the whole town is buzzing about you and that very attractive policeman, Ellie. You know how small towns are, by ten this morning we all knew exactly how long he stayed last night. No lights on upstairs while he was there, good for you. Whoring around with a man you hardly know is not the way to conduct yourself, not with two daughters."

The kettle whistled, and she turned and poured the steaming water into the teapot, picked up the teapot carefully, and swirled it gently. "I can't have you telling him about me, can I? I mean, that would lead to all sorts of questions, and frankly, I'm not in the mood right now. Let's give this a few minutes to steep, shall we?" She pulled out her chair and sat down, looking up at me expectantly. "Please, sit down, Ellie. And tell me, I hear your oldest daughter may be moving to France? I love France. Went there with Gerald years ago, when Lacey was in college. We had a wonderful time, although I must say Paris was not very friendly to us. I hear things have changed. I hope so for your daughter's sake."

I glanced at the doorway again. She was sitting, so if I ran, I might make it. Or not. If she caught me a second time, what could she do to me? I felt sure she would use more than her fist. She would try to kill me.

"I wouldn't tell Sam anything, Kate. You can trust me."

She tilted her head and looked very apologetic. "Oh, Ellie, if only I could be sure. But people are terrible liars. Lacey promised me she'd give me all the money that Gerald left her, but she didn't. She said the boys' money was in trust, but I didn't care. She promised me. I don't think she realized how serious I was, so I had to show her. Of course, I tried to get the boys, but I didn't know where Doug's sister lived. So I had to settle for Doug." She lifted the lid of the teapot and leaned over to inhale the steam. "Oh, this smells lovely. Shall I pour?"

I felt sick to my stomach. The pain in my cheek was keeping me focused. I glanced at the table. There was nothing there I could use as a weapon, no carelessly placed paring knife or heavy iron doorstop. I smiled. I could not afford to panic. I needed to do something. But what?

"Oh, wait, I have these lovely scones I made yesterday. Do you bake? I love to. Cookies are my specialty." She got up and moved, coming around the table and behind me. I instinctively hunched my shoulders. What if—

Something came down in front of my eyes and around my throat. I brought my hands up, but it was too late. It was one of the cotton towels, tightening around my neck. I could hear her behind me and feel her hands twisting the fabric. It was impossible to scream. I reached out, hoping for anything to use against her, and my fingers found the teapot. I grabbed the spout with one hand and the handle with the other, and swung my arms up and back, and the teapot smashed into her face. I felt the steaming tea splash against my hair and neck. She screamed, and in that second she broke her grip, and I lunged away from her, knocking over the table in front of me and tearing at my throat as I ran screaming through her living room and straight into Sam Kinali's arms.

"Are you okay?" he asked, his voice shaking.

I stared at him in surprise, then nodded.

"Are you sure? My God, Ellie, what did she do?"

Her tiny living room was full of dark uniforms. There were loud noises everywhere, and I felt cold. He moved away from me, and now the noises seemed far away too, and a very young man in a blue uniform lead me outside and sat me down on one of Kate's shiny white rocking chairs. He was asking me questions, I think, but I couldn't hear very well. Then another young man took his place, and a woman—she looked very kind—was looking in my eyes, and the young man was taking my pulse, and then I stopped shaking, and I could hear everything.

"What's your name, ma'am?" the woman asked.

"Ellie Rocca."

"Good. Now, Ellie, can you tell me what day it is?" The young man put something against my cheek, a cold pack that felt wonderful.

I could hear Kate screaming. Her voice was hoarse, and her words were vile, filthy. She was being taken from the house. I looked down. I could not watch her. "It's Saturday. May fifteenth."

"Good." Her fingers were against my neck, and the skin felt raw and burned. "What was this, a rope?" she asked.

I shook my head. "No. I think she used a tea towel." That suddenly struck me as very funny, and I started to laugh, and I was still laughing when Sam came up on the porch and pulled me up and against him.

Then I started to cry.

The paramedics determined that I did not need to go to the hospital. They gave me a shot of something that took away the pain in my cheek and cleaned my bloody nose. Shelly appeared from nowhere, had a long talk with Sam, then sat with me in the back of the patrol car that took me home. I immediately lay down on the couch. I was aware of Cait, looking horrified, and Tessa starting to cry, and then I was dreaming, odd bits and pieces, Lacey Mitchell and her little boys, waving.

When I awoke, I could tell by the shadows that it was past dinnertime. And I could smell pizza. My mouth felt numb, as did my cheek and eyes. I sat up slowly. My eye was swollen almost shut. My throat felt raw, on the inside and the outside. And I was starving.

"Hey," I called out. My voice sounded weak and strained.

Tessa came in first, running, but when she saw me, she stopped and started to cry. I held my arms out to her, and she crawled in.

Cait and Sam came in together, Cait sitting beside me, Sam across from us on the chair. I looked at Cait over Tessa's head.

"You should be at work."

She shook her head. "Mom, I should be here."

"No. Go to work. Tessa can take care of me. And Sam. You need the tips. Paris is expensive, remember?"

Sam smiled. "I told you, Cait. Go ahead. I can stay."

She looked at me, and her eyes filled with tears. "Are you going to be okay?"

I nodded. "Yes. Really. Go."

She got up and went upstairs. Tessa was down to just sniffles, so we sat there for a few more minutes. I was looking over her head at Sam.

"Thank you."

"For what? You had everything under control by the time I got there."

I shook my head. "She would have come after me. She would have chased me up one side of Davis Road and down the other."

"Perhaps. But I'm sure one of your neighbors would have noticed and at least tried to stop her."

"She's Millicent?"

He nodded.

"She's crazy," I said.

He shrugged. "According to Lacey, she's also evil."

"Lacey? You found Lacey?"

"She found us. She had been in a motel in Harrisburg, looking for a place for her family to relocate. When she heard about Doug, she drove back here. The plan was for him to try to keep things as normal for the boys as possible. He stayed with the boys, because according to her, he thought she was more likely to be in danger once the mother found them. He didn't think he'd be a target." He took a deep breath and shook his head. "She told us about her mother. That's why we happened to be there. We were coming to arrest her."

Tessa slid off my lap and looked up at me. "You look awful. Do you hurt?"

I nodded. "Yes. And I'm starving. Do I smell pizza?"

She brightened. "Yes. Do you want some?"

I nodded again. "Yes. On a tray, please. And water."

She bounced off the couch and was gone.

Sam was looking after her. "Your daughters are both very lovely. And quite entertaining."

I tried to smile. "I bet. Was Shelly here, or did I dream that?"

"Shelly left about half an hour ago. You slept for almost four hours. I have pain pills for you, if you need them. And Shelly said she could come back. With Maggie. And Carol. And just about everyone else in Mt. Abrams."

"She wanted the money," I said.

Sam nodded. "Yes. It was all about the money. She left her husband about ten years ago. No one ever knew where she was or what she was doing. We'll find out, of course. She returned to Fairfax just in time for her husband to die. They're reopening that case as well."

"She told me she killed him," I said. "Killed him for the money."

He looked thoughtful. "That's good to know, but I doubt you'll need to testify."

"She followed them back here?"

"Yes. When the will was read, she told Lacey she wanted her share. Lacey took off and came back here. She didn't realize her mother had tracked her down until she heard her voice in the library. She and Doug decided to give her the money and run. They handed over most of it to her, but they couldn't touch the trust."

"She told me. She said she tried to find the boys. She couldn't. She found Doug instead."

"Yes. I don't know what she said or did, but he allowed her to get in the car with him. That's where she stabbed him with an insulin injection. He probably had a seizure before he blacked out. Her fingerprints are everywhere. The autopsy results will confirm. We've got her."

I sighed. "Good."

"It was a very brave thing you did, Ellie," Sam said. He was speaking very carefully. "It was also very reckless. If you had any reason to suspect Kate was a killer, why did you go to see her?"

I looked away from him. "I just wanted to ask her a question. I didn't really *know*, I just..."

Tessa came back, carrying a tray very carefully. She set it down and watched as I sipped some water.

"Does it hurt to drink?" she asked.

I tried to smile. I kept forgetting I shouldn't. "A little. But Sam has pills for me."

I tried to eat the pizza, but it burned the inside of my mouth where my teeth had cut in. So I drank all the water, took two of the pills, and slept again.

I woke up once, in the middle of the night, to go to the bathroom. Tessa lay curled on the couch by my feet. Cait was asleep on the chair. And Sam was in my reading chair tucked in the corner. He was awake.

"How are you feeling?" he whispered.

I knelt down in front of him. "You should go home. I'm fine."

He brushed the hair off my face. "Do yourself a favor. Don't look in the mirror for a few days."

"Gee, thanks. I look that good?"

His eyes met mine. "You're beautiful."

I went to the bathroom, and of course, looked in the mirror. My eye was swollen shut, my cheek and jaw bruised purple, and lips and nose were puffy.

I took another pain pill and climbed back next to Tessa and fell asleep again, watching Sam watching me.

The next morning Sam was gone, and we were all tired and cranky and my entire face felt awful. Tessa attempted to start the morning with a cheerful, "Happy Mother's Day," but it fell a little flat. The good news was that Cait offered to get my mother from the nursing home. The bad news was three texts from Marc, wanting to know if he could come to brunch as well.

I had already bought tickets for the eleven o'clock seating, so that was an easy no. I wanted to blow off the Arboretum completely. This conversation needed more than texts.

I called Marc and told him what had happened. He immediately wanted to come over, but I put him off. If my mother did not remember the orchid show, we'd take her back to the home right after brunch. If she did remember, I'd give him a call.

I showered, put more ice on my face, and found a pretty scarf to put around my neck to hide the redness. I got texts from pretty much every person I knew, asking if I was all right. I drank hot tea with honey and waited for Caitlyn.

My mother took one look at my face and started to cry. "Why did he do this to you?"

I put my arms around her. "Mom, I'm fine. Who do you think did this to me?"

"Marc. Was he drunk? Has he hit you before?"

"Mom, Marc did not hit me. I fell. I'll be fine. Ready to go to brunch?"

She was still crying. "You have to leave him if he beats you. Even though he's such a nice boy."

I patted her back. Tessa and Cait were trying not to laugh. We got her as far as the porch when she started crying again.

"What will happen if he leaves? How will you live? Oh, dear, get a good lawyer." She wiped her eyes with the sleeve of her sweater.

Shelly, Mike, and their two boys saw us, and Shelly hurried over. "Ellie, what is it?" She peered at my mother. "Hi, Leona, remember me? What's wrong?"

Mike was looking at my face closely. "Wow, that crazy lady did a number on you," he said. I tried not to laugh because it hurt, but the situation was getting out of hand.

My mother was telling Shelly about my abusive husband, Marc, and how getting a divorce would send me out into the street. Shelly and Mike's kids wanted a closer look at my black eye, and Tessa was getting hungry. Mike managed to move us all, inches at a time, closer to the clubhouse, and my mother finally got distracted.

"Look," she said suddenly. "There's a sign over the door. Mother's Day! How exciting!"

We sat with Shelly and Mike, and had omelets and French toast, and I chewed all the bacon I could manage on the good side of my mouth. Of course, the entire population of Mt. Abrams knew the whole story of Lacey and Doug Mitchell, and my part in it all, and there was a seemingly endless stream of concerned friends and curious strangers stopping by for a word or six. My mother told all of them I would soon be divorcing, because well, look at her. Everyone smiled and nodded, and after an hour I was exhausted.

"What do you want to do now, Mom?" I asked her.

She patted her hair. "I know you wanted to see the orchids, but you look dead on your feet. Besides, if I have to look at that monster you're married to, I may do him violence. Cait, can you take me back?"

I was so grateful, I almost wept.

Cait and Mom walked back across Abrams Lane, and my mother waved as she got into Cait's car. Tessa and I had stopped to look out at the lake. It was beautiful, and I never tired of it. Tessa put her arms around my waist.

"It's pretty," she said.

"Yes."

"Mrs. Mitchell is back."

"I know." I had seen the Suburban parked in the drive earlier.

Shelly came over and stood with us. "You guys want to come over for the first cookout of the season?" she asked. "A day like this shouldn't be wasted."

I nodded gratefully. "Thanks. Yes, that would be great."

She poked me with her elbow. "You good?"

I nodded. "I will be."

Shelly smiled and followed her family down the hill.

"Mom, if you had a superpower, what would you want it to be?" Tessa asked.

I tightened my arm around her. "To be able to keep you and your sister safe forever."

She nodded. "That's a good one."

"Gee. Thanks. What would yours be?"

"To save all the good days, days like today, so when you were having bad days, you could take them out and live them all over again."

I watched in the distance as Lacey Mitchell came out of her house, got in her car, and drove away.

"That's a good one too, honey."

We turned away from the lake and walked home.

I called Marc again.

"I still love you, too," I said quietly. "But things are confusing right now."

"Your date?"

I nodded, then realized I was sitting on my porch, watching the sunset, with the dog on my lap, and Marc probably hadn't heard me nod. I cleared my throat and said, loudly, "Yes. I like him."

"If he's the one causing the confusion..." Marc began.

"But, he's not. You are."

"Oh," he said quietly.

Boot whined and snuggled in closer. I had managed without the painkillers all day, but knew I'd need them to sleep, and had taken the full dosage a few minutes earlier. I didn't think they'd go to work so quickly, but I felt a sudden heaviness, and my mind began to get fuzzy.

"Can we be friends?" I asked.

"Always."

"Good. I have to go now."

I could hear him breathing. I remembered when we first started dating, and listening to him breathe on the phone was something I'd do every night we were apart. I felt the phone slip into my lap, and I closed my eyes.

I heard Kate's voice, screaming, and then Sam was there, looking angry. Kate was smiling at me, pouring tea. Doug Mitchell was sitting across from me. His smile was fixed, and his skin was blue, and he appeared to be crying.

Sam was there again.

"Good drugs," I murmured. Sam laughed, and I turned towards him and fell asleep.